Y.O.L.O

You Only Live Once

★* I.J Hidee ★*

Y.O.L.O

Paperback edition published in 2021.

Author I.J Hidee

Edition and correction 2021 © I.J Hidee

The moral rights of the author have been asserted.

All rights reserved.

No part of this publication may be reproduced, stored in a retrieval system, or transmitted, in any form or by any means with prior permission, without prior permission in writing of the publishers, nor be otherwise circulated in any form of binding or cover other than that in which it is published and without a similar condition being imposed on the subsequent purchaser.

★* Y.O.L.O - I.J Hidee ★*

Live now. Regret later

★* Y.O.L.O - I.J Hidee ★*

★* Y.O.L.O series ★*

Book #1: Y.O.L.O - You Only Live Once

Book #2: W.O.L.O - We Only Live Once

Book #3: Coming soon

★* Y.O.L.O - I.J Hidee ★*

★* Y.O.L.O - I.J Hidee ★*

Prologue

The policemen chased us down the busy streets, but the air was filled with laughter.

"Come on, Carter, you're too slow!" Killian snickered. He gave me a gentle push forward. I almost lost my balance. It was hard enough for me to run in a skirt, especially since I was a boy who grew up wearing pants. It was my first time crossdressing, not that it was much of a choice.

"If you don't hurry, we'll get caught!" Francisco chuckled. They seemed too cheerful for two boys being chased by the police. Killian wore a wide, confident grin and looked unbothered by the gravity of our situation. He looked like he was enjoying the thrill rather than fearing it.

Anyone could tell that this wasn't his first time committing a crime, nor would it be his first if he got caught. As his partner in crime, I found that both deeply worrisome and slightly reassuring.

Killian quickened his pace and ran ahead of me. It was as if he was born to run. The wind brushed through his silky, dark hair, his strong arms pushed him forward, and his calves strengthened at each footfall. He looked so free and full of life.

★* Y.O.L.O - I.J Hidee ★*

He looked over his shoulder, his bright pistachio-colored eyes glistening under the daylight. A smile grew at the corner of his lips, revealing his pearly white teeth. I wondered what toothpaste he used. Colgate? Crest? Elmex maybe?

"Carter," he called. "Take my hand."

He extended his arm, and I could see the four letters tattooed on his knuckles. Y.O.L.O.

"Well?" he laughed, snapping me out of my trance.

Before I knew it, I reached out to hold his hand. The wind knocked out my breath and a burning pain hurt my thighs, but I pushed myself to exceed my limits. The tip of my fingers brushed against his. He grabbed my hand and our fingers intertwined.

Now running side by side, we ran down the crowded streets, ignoring the shouts and stares, laughing and hooting like there was no tomorrow.

We didn't know what would happen next, but we kept going forward without looking back. Why?

Because Y.O.L.O.

★* Y.O.L.O - I.J Hidee ★*

Chapter 1: Nine Lives

"Why do cats have nine lives while humans only have one?" Eshe hummed, drumming her fingers against the plump of her cheek. It was a bright and sunny afternoon, but despite the perfect weather, my best friend and I stayed inside to prepare for next week's test.

"It's a proverb, Eshe," I said, trying to solve the math equation without getting distracted by her wandering thoughts.

"That doesn't answer my question," she pouted.

"Cats are incredibly intelligent and intuitive animals."

"Still doesn't answer my question," Eshe sang.

"Cats are worshipped in various countries, and there's a superstition in some cultures that the number nine brings luck and fortune."

"My question remains unanswered," she chirped. I put my pencil down and finally looked up from my textbook.

"You just want to hear me say 'I don't know,' don't you?"

A wide smile grew on Eshe's face.
"It's not every day that you hear the school's genius say those three magical words."

My eyes fell back to the numbers scribbled on my notebook.

"I'm not a genius," I mumbled quietly. "I work hard, that's all."

"What the difference?"

The *difference was* that I spent days and nights studying to be on the same par as the real geniuses born with photographic memories and high IQs. The *difference was* that I had to sacrifice hours of my free time to keep straight A's on my report card. The *difference was* that I had to double my efforts to get into the same universities as the gifted prodigies of our school. But of course, I didn't mention any of the above.

I decided to take a break from the advanced algebra equations. We've been studying for two solid hours. I felt like brain was going to combust.

"You work too hard and study too much," she said. My parents would say otherwise, but again, I kept my the thought to myself, which was a miracle considering that I had a bad habit of letting my tongue slip.

"Says the girl who spent eight hours finishing her science project."

She didn't deny it.

"Is giving this much homework even legal?" she sighed. "I feel like a robot. It doesn't even feel like we're living."

"We are living," I said.

"Are we?"

"We are."

Just in a very boring way.

"You did it again," she noted, and I realized that I said my thoughts out loud this time.

"Sorry."

"Well, you aren't wrong. But hey, look on the bright side. Once we graduate high school and get a Ph.D. degree and a job that pays six figures, we can have as much fun as we want," she said, giving me a gentle nudge. "Plus, we'll be filthy rich."

"We'll be over thirty by then," I frowned.

"Over thirty, but happy," she reminded me, raising her cup of milk. We toasted to our happy thirties.

We spent the rest of the afternoon studying. When the sun went down, Eshe had to leave, but I continued studying until my parents called me down for dinner at 7:00 p.m. I didn't have to check the time to know.

I woke up at seven a.m, went to school at 8:00 a.m, came home at 5:00 p.m, and studied until 7:00 p.m which was when my parents came home from work. I wasn't living life. I was living a routine.

I tried to cheer myself up. Even if I wasn't living my best life now, I'd be free to do whatever I wanted later, right?

"Did anything exciting happen at school today?" Mom asked, snapping me out of my thoughts. The muscles in my cheeks pulled.

"No, nothing happened," I said. Nothing ever did.

***

"Are you okay?" Eshe asked, joining me at my lockers. "You look like you didn't get a wink of sleep."

"I spent the entire night studying for our history test," I mumbled, rubbing my tired eyes.

"Didn't you finish studying for that like a week ago?" she asked, fixing my floppy brown hair.

I didn't bother brushing my hair this morning so that I could lay in bed a little longer. Those few extra minutes didn't seem like much, but they were precious. Besides, no one was going to notice my bed hair anyway. Nerds like me were never the center of attention, so I didn't have to worry about my looks. There wasn't anyone I was trying to impress either.

"I forgot a chapter."

★* Y.O.L.O - I.J Hidee ★*

"You should have slept," she frowned.

And risk missing a question? Not possible.

"Carter, you can't keep pulling all-nighters," she murmured softly. "You're already so small and frail."

I was wearing a size M, but it looked like an XL on my scrawny body. I fixed my crooked glasses.

"I'm not that small," I argued, puffing up my chest.

"Sweetie, you're tiny."

I deflated.

"Men don't like it when they're called tiny."

"You're a baby," she laughed, poking my arm. "A small bean."

I looked nothing like the tall jocks who strut down the halls wearing strong-scented cologne. I smelled like baby powder, and my chin was nowhere near the tusk of manhood.

"Are you sure you're not going to fall asleep halfway through the test?"

My mouth wanted to say yes, but my brain was saying a hard no.

"I'll buy a soda," I said. "The sugar will keep me awake for the next hour."

"Do you need money?"

"Don't worry, I have spare change," I smiled. Eshe didn't seem to like the idea of me depending on sugar to survive the rest of the day, but she knew I'd be in an even worse state if I didn't get an A+.

"I'll wait for you in the classroom," she said.

I nodded and headed to the closest vending machine. I inserted the coins and punched E3 for the cherry-flavored soda. The machine made a loud whirring noise, but the soda stopped moving. I shook the machine, but it wouldn't fall forward.

"Please come out," I begged. "I need to drink you."

A soft ripple of laugher came from behind and I spun around in surprise. A tall boy stood behind me. He looked familiar, but with my severe lack of sleep and panicking mind, my sluggish mind couldn't put a name on his handsome face.

The first thought that popped in my mind was, *he's gorgeous*. The second thought was, *I should have brushed my hair this morning*. The last one was, *I'm going to fail my test*. Normally, the order should have been reversed.

He was tall, so I had to crane my neck to meet his gaze. He had an intimidating, sharp jaw, and dark, brown hair. His eyes were the brightest pair of green I've ever seen. They looked like a color that didn't exist. With just one look, I knew he was one of the popular kids. The confident grin and natural charisma said it all.

★* Y.O.L.O - I.J Hidee ★*

"Trying to rip someone off again?" he asked.

I blinked, and realized he wasn't talking to me, but the machine. He shoved his large hands into his jean pockets, and for a second, I thought he was going to leave. My jaw dropped open when he kicked the machine like it was some kind of soccer ball. The machine shook from the impact and made a terrifying screeching noise as if something was dying inside of it. I frantically looked around us, but the handsome boy and I were the only ones in the hallway.

The machine finally stopped screaming, followed by two loud clinks. The boy slipped his hand into the slot and pulled out two cans of cherry soda. When he handed me one, I noticed that his knuckles were tattooed. They looked like letters, but he pulled away before I could read it.

"To broken machines and cute boys who don't know how to use them," he said, raising his can and clinking it against mine.

A wave of heat flushed my cheeks. Before I could thank him, the bell rang, and he had already left.

Chapter 2: It's just…

"Killian Henderson?" Mr. Clyde called.

"That's him!" I gasped. Heads turned around and I stiffened, realizing that I had voiced out my thoughts. Our history teacher raised a brow and I chuckled nervously.

"Sorry," I apologized sheepishly.

Mr. Clyde scanned the room.

"Absent as usual," he grumbled

I couldn't believe that I didn't recognize the school's most popular bad boy. Calling him a bad boy was cringey, but that was what he was. He did whatever he wanted, whenever he wanted, however he wanted. The only rules he cared about were his own.

If I had to describe him in some cheesy romance novel, it'd probably go something like this:

Killian Henderson, a mysterious boy with unruly hair and beautiful emerald eyes. He has a jawline that could cut wood, a perfectly symmetrical face, nice thick brows, and is a total hunk from head to toe. He acts like a total jerk, rebellious and daring, but deep down, he's a sentimental boy struggling with his own problems that push him to act bad. That is, until a beautiful, sweet girl changes his life and makes him want to be good ill love fail or prevail?

I gave myself a self-satisfactory pat on the back. I could write my own book.

"Carter Jones," Mr. Clyde called. I raised my hand to answer, but he didn't even look up from his clipboard. "Here as always."

Everyone knew Carter Jones didn't miss a day of school. If I was known for something, it was for my perfect attendance. It's been like that since, well, forever.

Now, I know what you're thinking, but let me stop you right there. You're probably thinking, 'Oh, Carter is the sweet, innocent goodie-two-shoes who's going to change the bad boy.'

Wrong. Incorrecto. Nada possible.

Excuse my broken Spanish, but I took German.

I was a good, hardworking honor student, but there was no way that Killian and I would ever get involved with each other. Why? First of all, he never came to class while I *only* came to class. Besides, there was no way I'd fall for him and there was an even smaller chance that he'd fall for me. He was the school's most popular student, and I was just a nerd. On top of that, we were both *boys*. The only rumors I've heard about him exclusively involved girls.

"To broken machines and cute boys."

His husky voice echoed inside my mind. My cheeks unexpectedly grew hot, and I bit my lower lip. I quickly pushed away his voice.

No, I was Carter Jones, you're supposed to be the good boy who stays away from the bad! That's how things are and that's how things were going to be.

***

When the teacher finished roll call, he asked us to clear our desks. We could keep our pencil case, but nothing else. He handed out the test sheets, and I bit back a smile when I saw the questions related to chapter 8, the one I spent the entire night revising. With a can of cherry soda bubbling inside my stomach and the sugar running through my veins, I felt better than ever.

I finished the test fives minutes early which gave me enough time to re-read my answers. I mentally had to stop myself from changing my answers and only corrected the few grammar mistakes. Whenever I changed an answer before handing in my paper, I always ended up regretting it.

"Carter? Can you collect the papers?" Mr. Clyde asked.

I walked down the rows. I told myself I needed to thank Killian but bumping into him this morning was like a Christmas miracle. Well, instead of meeting an old grandpa with a beer belly, I met a gorgeous boy with gorgeous eyes.

How was I going to thank him? We didn't hang out with the same crowd. Correction, *he* hung out with a crowd. I stuck with Eshe, my only friend at school. Besides, even if I saw Killian in the hallways, I doubt I'd have the courage to walk up to him, let alone, talk to him.

I went to my lockers. The sugar rush was starting to die down, and my exhaustion was catching up.

"Carter!" Eshe exclaimed, tackling me with a hug.

"Eshe," I gasped.

"Yes, Carty?" She batted her naturally long lashes that swept over her flawless, dark skin while squeezing the life out of me. A wide smile grew across her face, hinting that she did good on the test, and a string of curly hair fell over her forehead.

"No running in the halls," I winced. She released me, crossing her arms over her chest with narrowed eyes.

"Really? I come running to you with all my love and affection and all you have to say is 'no running in the halls?'" she huffed. "This is why you don't have a girlfriend."

"I don't need a girlfriend. I have you," I smiled sheepishly.

Lots of people thought we were dating, but Eshe and I were just best friends. I don't think she'd ask me which color of granny panties looked best on her if she liked me romantically.

She linked her arm around mine and we walked down the hall together. We discussed yesterday's English test, complaining about how hard the questions were and how we thought we were going to get a poor grade when we both knew that we would most likely get an A.

Yeah, we were *those* types of people.

We went to the cafeteria and the cafeteria lady served us spaghetti and meatballs. Well, what I assuming was spaghetti and meatballs.

"Oh right, did you hear about the latest school scandal?"

"Which one?

"The one about Killian," she said.

My ears perked. "Killian Henderson?" I asked, suddenly curious.

"No, Killian Bonapart," she said with an eye roll. "Yes, Killian Henderson."

"What did he do?" I prompted. "Are you falling for him too?"

"Too?" she inquired.

"Too as in all the other girls at school," I quickly said. "Not me. Definitely not me."

Eshe gave me a weird stare but shrugged.

"He's not my type," she simply said. "Besides, it doesn't seem like he swings that way."

★* Y.O.L.O - I.J Hidee ★*

"What way?"

"The straight way."

I blinked in surprise.

"Rumors have it that he was caught doing the dirty deeds with another guy in the boy's locker room."

"What?" I coughed.

"Yeah, apparently it was with Luke, the captain of the football team," she whispered. Weren't Killian and Luke best friends? "People say Killian was sucking—"

Eshe wasn't looking where she was going and bumped into someone. The cup of water on her tray fell and soaked the person's shoe.

"I'm so—" she stopped when she saw who it was.

Desiree was the captain of the cheerleading team and one of the most popular girls in school. The guys in my class would often talk about her, ranking her in their top three to do lists, because apparently, girls were no different than chores to them.

Desiree was wearing a mini skirt and a top that showed too much cleavage, violating the school's dress code. But she never seem to care because it never stopped her from wearing what she wanted. That was one of the few things I liked about her, and probably the only thing I liked about her.

"Are you kidding me?" she screeched in her bratty voice.

"I didn't see you," Eshe mumbled, forgetting her apology.

"Do you know how expensive these shoes are?" Desiree snapped. "Oh right, someone as poor as you probably wouldn't know."

Eshe pursed her lips, her cheeks flushing pink with embarrassment.

"Desiree, it's just water," I frowned. "It'll dry off."

She looked at me as if she just noticed me. A sneer touched her lips.

"And you are?" she prompted with no real interest. I shrunk.

"Carter," I replied in a small voice.

"What's that, pipsqueak? You're mumbling." I opened my mouth to say something, but she raised her hand to stop me. "Look, it's nice of you to try and be the knight in shining armor, but it doesn't really work when you're as short as a dwarf and as thin as a twig."

"Hey, back off," Eshe said, but Desiree pinched her nose.

"Ew, don't come any closer. I don't want to breathe same air as you."
Apparently, she didn't know how oxygen worked.

"Oh, that does it," Eshe growled. "Carty, hold my hoops!"

She placed her earrings on my tray. Before I could stop them, Desiree and Eshe started fighting. A crowd gathered around us, hooting and encouraging them to fight. Desiree grabbed a bottle of apple juice and splashed it in Eshe's face. The room went dead silent. Desiree let out a fake gasp, putting a hand over her mouth in shock.

"Oops," Desiree pouted. "But it's just apple juice, right? It'll dry off."

Eshe was mad. No, she was *furious*. Before she could break Desiree's nose job, someone dumped a plate of spaghetti over Desiree's head, and she let out an ear-piercing scream as noodles and meatballs dribbled down her face.

"Whoops," Killian smiled innocently, holding the empty plate. "It's just spaghetti, right?"

★* Y.O.L.O - I.J Hidee ★*

Chapter 3: Pistachio Eyes

I jumped in my chair when the principal slammed his fists against his desk.

"Someone explain to me why one of my students is covered in spaghetti," Mr. Rodriguez ordered. The four of us were sent to his office and sat on the chairs that looked like execution chairs. "You, you, you, and *you*," he glowered, emphasizing the former when pointing at Killian. "Are in big trouble. I want an explanation. *Now*."

Killian smiled. "Well, I'd be more than happy to—"

"No, not you. Anyone but you," he hissed.

"Relax, Mr. Roro, you're gonna bust a vein."

Desiree stepped in before Mr. Rodriguez could flip his desk.

"It wasn't Killian's fault," she said. "I was looking for my friends in the cafeteria until Eshe suddenly dumped water on my shoes."

"You have friends?" Eshe snorted. Killian masked his laughter with a cough.

"She deliberately ruined my shoes!" Desiree cried, raising her leg to show us her damp shoes. Mr. Rodriguez leaned forward and squinted his eyes.

"What exactly am I supposed to be looking at?"

"Water," she huffed.

"Girl, put your stanky shoe down. You're embarrassing all four of us," she said, pushing Desiree's leg down.

"Eshe didn't do it on purpose. It was an accident," I said.

"She did do it on purpose, *nerd*," Desiree snapped back.

"Hey, don't call him that," Eshe hissed.

"Why not?"

"Oh, because honey, I have a million nicknames for you, and you don't want to hear a single one of them."

War was hailed. The girls argued and shouted, and I shrunk in my seat, scared that the ceiling might crumble. Killian yawned loudly. That was it. He just yawned.

"Enough!" Mr. Rodriguez boomed. He pinched the inner corner of his eyes and took in a deep breath. "Aside from the water accident, who dumped a plate of spaghetti on Desiree's head? Because you can't tell me that that was an accident."

The room fell silent. Eshe and I didn't want to snitch on Killian. To our surprise, Killian voluntarily raised his hand.

"That would be me."

"Why." It didn't sound like a question.

"'Cause I felt like it." Killian's voice didn't come off haughty or arrogant. He was simply stating a fact.

My lips parted in shock. Was he out of his mind?!

"Mr. Henderson, I'm sure you are aware that this isn't the first time you've broken the school rules. I'm going to call your mother and discuss your unacceptable behavior."
I noticed that Killian's jaw ticked when Mr. Rodriguez mentioned his mom. It was the first time I've seen him look uneasy.

"Consider yourself suspended until further notice," Mr. Rodriguez snapped curtly, pulling out a suspension sheet. "The rest of you may leave."

Desiree frowned. "But sir—"

"Would you like to be suspended as well?"

Desiree flinched and her voice fell to a whisper. "No, sir."

"Good. The three of you may leave my office," he said, pointing at the door with the back of his pen. The girls headed for the door, but I remained seated, squeezing my clammy hands together. A hundred thoughts ran through my mind.
"Carter?" Mr. Rodriguez prompted. "Is something wrong?"

I must be crazy. I really must be crazy.

"Carter?" he repeated a little louder.

"Mr. Rodriguez, I was the one who told Killian to dump the plate of spaghetti on Desiree. It was supposed to be a joke, but I guess it wasn't as funny as I thought."

All eight pairs of eyes were now on me, but the one that made me the most nervous was Killian's. It stressed me out whenever a handsome guy looked at me. I knew what suspension would cost him. Killian would either have to take summer classes or re-do his entire year. But if Mr. Rodriguez took my bluff and suspended Killian, then he'd have to suspend me too. He wouldn't do that to one of the best students in his school, right?

But if my plan didn't work, then my long-lived efforts to keep a perfect academic record would go down the drain in seconds. Worst of all, I'd have to face my parents.

"Did Killian ask you to take the blame?" Mr. Rodriguez asked sternly. No, I owed him for this morning.

"He didn't," I said with more confidence.
After a dreadfully long pause, the principal let out a long sigh.

"Carter, I am very disappointed in you," he said, and I flinched. He put the suspension slip back into his drawer. I felt relieved until he said, "I won't suspend Killian because it would be unfair if I only punished one of you two. But you and Mr. Henderson will be spending the next two months in detention."

My heart dropped when I heard the word detention.

Never in my life would I have thought I'd get detention. I was supposed to be the good kid. No, I *was* the good kid. Getting detention was like sending me to prison!

Mr. Rodriguez dismissed us. I left his office feeling like I had left my soul in there. I looked up from the floor and stiffened when my eyes met Killian's. He was staring at me, and he didn't even try to hide it.

His green eyes held a vivid color of mischief and vivacity. Grass green, bright emeralds, spring leaves, all those adjectives fit them, but pistachio-green described them best. Plus, pistachios were my favorite type of nut. His eyes had the same crisp brown and the same bright green hidden within the shells.

My body tensed when he leaned towards me, lowering his head to my height. I got a whiff of his divine shampoo. I expected him to thank me or say a word of gratitude, but all I got was a curious sentence that left me confused.

"I'll see you in detention, Jones," he whispered in a husky voice, low enough for only me to hear. He flashed me a smile before sauntering off. I stood there wide-eyed and in a daze.

How did he know my last name?

★* Y.O.L.O - I.J Hidee ★*

Chapter 4: Chicken v.s Wolf

Class ended and it was time for detention. Eshe rushed to my desk as soon as the bell rang.

"Carter, why?" she demanded, pressing the flat of her palms against my desk.

"I don't know," I said miserably.

"You shouldn't have taken the blame for something you didn't do."

"I felt bad for him. He was trying to help us," I frowned.

"We didn't ask him to do anything. You heard him! He did it because *he* wanted to."

I didn't answer.

"I should have said something to Mr. Rodriguez. No, we still have time. Let's go to his office and—"

"No," I blurted. Eshe stared at me quizzically and I felt my face redden. "If we go now, then he'll know that I lied."

"It's better than getting detention!"

"I can handle detention, don't worry." Before she could say anything else, I quickly said, "I have to hurry, or I'll be late."

She pursed her lips sideways.

"Come back alive, Carty."

I smiled weakly. "I'll try."

"And be careful around Killian. I don't trust him. And if he so much as lays a finger on you—"

"Don't worry, I can take care of myself," I reassured her, but Eshe didn't seem convinced. When I turned around the corner, my shoulder bumped into something hard. I staggered back and almost lost my balance.

"What where you're going, nerd," someone snapped harshly.

I stiffened when I recognized Luke's voice. His cold, blue eyes narrowed on me, and I dropped my gaze. He was the captain of our school's football team, so it was no surprise that his bold shoulders felt like steel.

Wait, didn't Eshe say that he was caught doing the dirty deeds with Killian?

"What are you staring at?" he snapped.

"Sorry," I stammered.

He clicked his tongue and walked past me. Luke was known for his bad mood swings, but his aggressiveness helped on the field. I went to the detention room and stopped at the door. My P.E teacher, Mr. Yon, was sitting at the front desk with his feet on the table. There was a bag of chips perched on his belly.

"Hello, Mr. Yon," I squeaked. He didn't look up from his magazine.

"Hello, student," he replied. He gestured towards the chairs. "Take a seat. There aren't many left."

I stared at the empty classroom and then realized he was being sarcastic. I laughed a beat too late and before things got any more awkward, I sat down near the window.

Where was Killian? Would he even bother showing up? Who ditches detention? Oh, right. Killian.

Detention wasn't as bad as I had thought. It felt like I had my own private room to study in. It was way better than having to fight for a seat in the school library. The science kids were the worst. They fought for a table as if their braces depended on it.

I finished my homework and started studying for next week's science test, using flashcards to help me memorize the jargon of complicated words. My ears perked up when I heard the door squeak open.

"Ah, Killian, you showed up," Mr. Yon snorted, still flipping through his magazine. He was thirty minutes late.

"If you're lucky, you might find a seat."

★* Y.O.L.O - I.J Hidee ★*

The class was empty.

"Then I guess today's my lucky day," he beamed. His eyes locked on mine before I could look away. He sat down beside me. The entire classroom was filled with empty seats, why did he have to choose the one right beside me?!

I switched flashcards and tried to focus, but Killian's presence made me nervous. Why did I get the feeling that he was staring at me? My eyes shifted towards him, and I yelped at how close his face was. I jerked back to put some distance between us.

"What are you doing?" I hissed.

"Sorry, didn't mean to scare you," he chuckled. "You were just so focused on your flashcards that I thought you were reading a porno magazine or something."

He picked up the pencil I dropped. When he moved, I got a quick whiff of his scent. He smelled nice.

"Here," he said.

"Thanks," I murmured, taking the pencil. I noticed that he had four letters tattooed on his knuckles. Y.O.L.O.

"You like it?" Killian smiled, flipping his hand so I could get a better look. "It's my life philosophy."

I scowled. *Your life philosophy is based on a cringey, overused acronym?*

He laughed and I quickly slapped my hands over my mouth, but it was already too late.

"Sorry, I didn't mean to say it like that," I said. "But doesn't Y.O.L.O stand for you only live once?"

To my surprise, he didn't seem mad at all. In fact, he looked happy that I asked.

"Yeah," he nodded. He then studied me and pursed his lips with a playful look in his eyes. "But someone like you wouldn't understand."

"What's that supposed to mean?"

"Aren't you Carter Jones?" he inquired.

"Yes."

"The guy who ranks first in our class."

I nodded.

"The one who hardly has any friends, spends his free time studying, and who follows every rule that exists including the rules that probably don't?"

I snapped my head back in surprise. Wait, what?

He grinned. "I bet the most exhilarating thing you've done in your life is riding your bike without a helmet."

"That's not true!" I've never ridden my bike without my helmet. I wasn't suicidal, thank you very much.

Killian leaned on the heel of his chair, resting his hands behind his head. He looked at the ceiling.

"Let's face it, Jones. You live a safe but boring life, the complete opposite of my life's philosophy," he said. He glanced at me, and a smile quirked on his lips. "That's why I said you wouldn't understand."

"That's not true. And can you please stop doing that?" I asked, pushing his chair forward so all four legs were on the ground. He raised a brow, and I averted his gaze.

"It was making me nervous. What if you fall and hurt your head?"

Killian blinked blankly before bursting into laughter. I sank in my chair, feeling my cheeks redden.

"What about you?" I huffed, turning the tables. "Y.O.L.O doesn't mean living a reckless and irresponsible life."

"Irresponsible?" he gasped with a smile.

"Yes, irresponsible. You almost never come to class, and when you do, you're asleep."

"I didn't know you paid attention to me. Why didn't you tell me you were interested?" I knew he was just teasing me, but why did I feel butterflies in my chest?

"It's harder than you think, living the way I do," he said, waving his hand dismissively. I snorted,

"Doing whatever you want, whenever you want, however you want, is hard?" I challenged.

"Yup," he said in a heartbeat.

"I'll tell you what's hard. Pulling all-nighters to finish assignments, getting to class on time, never missing school, finishing homework even when you're sick, that's what's hard."

"Then let's make a bet," Killian smiled.

"A bet?" I asked.

"Four dares. You give me four dares to convince me that your lifestyle is harder than mine, and I'll give you four dares to show you how hard it is to live life like you only have one."

"I don't know," I mumbled reluctantly. I hardly knew Killian. Besides, who knew what he did in his free time? He could be a part-time serial killer for all I knew!

"Chickening out already?" he asked.

"I'm not chickening out. I just think it's a bad idea."

"What, having fun?" he snorted.

I narrowed my eyes, but he shrugged.

"Then I guess I'm right. Living my life is harder than yours."

I frowned. "No, it's just that—"

"You're too chicken to step out of your comfort zone?" he finished. I flinched.

"Do you hear that?" he gasped.

"Hear what?"

There was no one else in the classroom except us and our P.E teacher, but Mr. Yon was already sound asleep. Killian leaned closer towards me.

"I think I hear a chicken," Killian whispered. My eyebrows pulled together.

"I don't hear—"

"Bwak," he clucked. I stared at him, bewildered, then narrowed my eyes.

"That's real mature of you."

"Do you hear that? It's getting louder. Bwak, bwak," he squawked, putting his hands on his sides and flapped his arms. My jaw tightened.

"You're being—"

"Bwak," he cut me off.

"Killian—"

"Bwakkity, bwak, bwak," he sang.

"That's not even what a chicken—"

"Bwaaaak."

I tightened my fists. "Ki—"

"Bwak, buk, bacawk! Buk-"

"Alright, I'll take the bet! Just please stop making those unbearable chicken noises," I begged.

The second I saw the smile on his face, I knew I was doomed. He gave out his left hand.

"Then let's shake on it," he said. When I didn't answer right away, he said, "Don't chicken out on me, Jones. You're braver than that."

I bit my lower lip, then sighed. What was the worst that could happen?

So, I took his hand, and we shook on it.

★* Y.O.L.O - I.J Hidee ★*

Chapter 5: A Man-to-man Secret

My mom called me for dinner. I closed my notebook and headed downstairs. My parents didn't know that I got detention, and I wasn't planning on telling them. I served myself a plate of hot potatoes and drowned them in gravy.

"Don't you want any chicken with that?" Dad asked. I stiffened.

"Um, no thanks, I'm good," I chuckled stiffly.

"How was school?" Mom asked, taking a bite of her salad. Before I could answer, she said, "Did you get the results for your English test?"

I nodded and took a bite of my potato. I yelped when I burnt my tongue.

"Carter, you know those potatoes just got out of the oven," Dad sighed. "And yet you still burn yourself."

I bit my tongue between my teeth to make sure it was still there.

"We got our tests back," I finally said.

★* Y.O.L.O - I.J Hidee ★*

"Did you get a good grade?" Mom asked.

"A+."

A bright smile grew across her face. It was the first time she smiled since I got home.

"Aren't we so lucky to have such a brilliant child?" she gushed, putting her hand over dad's. "He reminds me of us when we were in high school."

I smiled awkwardly, staring at my plate. It was nice being praised by my parents, but it was always the same compliments that revolved around my academic achievements.

"Don't forget to study for your science test," Mom reminded me.

"Don't worry," I reassured her, poking my food. Life was becoming as plain as a potato. I needed some gravy to give it some flavor.

"Something crazy happened at lunch today," I said, hoping to get a reaction. "Eshe and I—"

"Carter, could you pass me the pepper?" Mom interrupted. I frowned but handed her the pepper. I tried again.

"There's a girl in our school named Desiree. Today she—"

"Is she smart?"

I furrowed my brows. "Um…"

"Is she pretty?" Dad asked.

"Paul!" Mom gasped, casting him a sharp glare. "Girls who waste time on anything other than their studies aren't a good influence. They should be studying for tests instead of coating their eyelashes with mascara."

"Why can't they do both?" I asked curiously.

"Beauty comes from within," she said, waving her fork dismissively. "If you're looking for a girlfriend, why don't you ask Eshe out?"

"Mom," I groaned, feeling my cheeks flush red. "I told you, Eshe is just a friend. She's like a sister to me. Besides, I'm not looking for a girlfriend right now."

"It's such a shame though. Eshe is such a good girl. She's smart and pretty too," Mom said encouragingly.

She's been Eshe's biggest fan since she won first place in our town's spelling bee. When I was a kid, my mom chose my friends for me. She was picky with most, but she'd always say yes whenever it was Eshe.

"Anyway," I said, trying to get back to what I was saying, but my parents had already changed the subject and were discussing something that happened at work. I felt like the only time they paid attention to me was when I was talked about my grades. Everything else didn't seem to matter.

"I'm going upstairs," I said, pushing my chair back.

"Already? You've hardly touched your food," Mom frowned.

"I'm not that hungry." Mom was about to protest, but I said, "I have to go study."

She let me go. I went to my room and closed the door. I pressed my back against the wall and sank to the floor. I knew my parents loved me, but sometimes it felt suffocating. There was an empty feeling inside of me.

I climbed onto my bed and wrapped my arms around my teddy bear, Panda. And yes, I named my stuffed teddy bear Panda. I checked my phone and my eyes brightened when I saw that I had an unread message. I knew who it was from before opening it.

Alix: Hey, Carter, are you free?

Me: Yeah, I just finished eating dinner.

Alix: Did your parents ask about your grades again?

Me: Yeah···

Alix: You okay?

Me: Yeah.

I jumped when my phone started to ring. I quickly lowered the volume and hid under the sheets so no one could hear me. I wasn't allowed to call anyone on school days unless it was for an emergency, but I could never turn down a call from my childhood best friend. We didn't get to talk to each other that much ever since he moved away.

"Hello?" I squeaked.

"Hey, Carter." I smiled as soon as I heard his voice.

"Why did you call?"

"I wanted to check up on you. Eshe texted and told me what happened. Did you really get detention?"

"Hm? Oh, yeah, I did, but it's not as bad as you think."

"Eshe mentioned a guy named Kill something?"

I giggled. "Killian."

"Isn't he that popular guy who's always ditching class?"

"Yeah, that's him."

"He didn't bother you in detention, did he?" Alix asked slowly.

I shook my head as if Alix was in front of me. "No, he didn't do anything."

"And it's just the two of you in detention?" He asked.

"There's also Mr. Yon, our P.E teacher." I paused. "Well, kind of. He fell asleep halfway through detention."

"You should be careful around him."

"Around Mr. Yon?" I asked.

"No, Killian."

I frowned. "Oh."
"You shouldn't trust guys like him. They do things for their own amusement. Who knows what he'll do to you just to

get a good laugh?" Alix said sternly. I guess this wasn't the best time to mention our bet.

"Don't worry, I can take care of myself," I said proudly. "We only see each other in detention, and he probably won't even come the next time."

Alix was probably raking a hand through his blond hair the way he did whenever he was uneasy.

"I just don't want you to get hurt," he murmured.

"Then come back," I teased with a small smile.

"You know I want to."

"When will you visit?"

"Probably not until winter break."

My heart fell to my stomach. "Oh."

There was a small pause.

"But hey, when I do come over, we'll do everything you want. We can even go to our favorite lake, just like the good old days," Alix said eagerly.

"The lake will be frozen by then," I chuckled softly.

"It'll still be fun. We can skate on the ice or something," he beamed.

"Yeah, that sounds fun," I smiled.

"I miss you, Carter."

The sudden stern tone of his voice surprised me. Before I could answer, I heard footsteps outside my door.

"I have to go now, bye!" I whispered, frantically hanging up. Dad opened the door, and I quickly came out of the covers, hiding my phone under my thigh. He narrowed his eyes suspiciously.

"What were you doing?" he asked slowly.

"I, um, I was…" I couldn't think of a lie. "Please don't tell Mom," I blurted. His eyes widened, and I stiffened. Did he hear me talking to Alix? Was he going to tell Mom? Were they going to confiscate my phone?

The wrinkles on his face softened.

"I see," he contemplated. Then the hardened expression on his face softened. "Don't worry, son," he said, the sudden change of attitude making my brows slowly draw together. "It's only natural for a boy your age."

I blinked in confusion.

"What?" I asked bluntly.

"Don't worry, I won't tell your mother. It'll be a man-to-man secret," he chuckled. "Oh, and you might want to use those."

He nodded towards the box of tissues beside my bed and my eyes widened in horror as I finally understood. My face

★* Y.O.L.O - I.J Hidee ★*

turned as red as a tomato as I snapped my head back towards him.

"Wait, Dad, it's not what you think!"

He put his hand up, stopping me.

"Now, now, there's no need to get all flustered. I didn't see a thing," he winked, closing the door before I could say anything else. I sat there in utter shock before groaning in embarrassment.

This had to be the worst.

Chapter 6: The First Dare

I was in history class, but I couldn't focus on what the teacher was saying. The embarrassment from last night was killing me. I also couldn't stop thinking about what Alix said to me about Killian. Was he really a bad person?

I rested my chin on my palm and looked out the window. My eyes widened in surprise when I saw Killian and Luke outside the school gates. They were ditching class together, but there was someone else with them. I could tell that he wasn't from our school since he was wearing a fancy school uniform that only students in private schools wore.

Whoever he was, he seemed close with them, especially Luke. The tall Asian boy casually put his arm around Luke, whispering something into his ear and making him laugh. My eyes fluttered in surprise, and I blinked hard to make sure I wasn't seeing things.

It was the first time I've seen Luke smile like that. The traces of his grouchy scowl and intimidating gaze were gone. I was surprised he didn't push the boy's arm off him. He always seemed annoyed whenever the cheerleaders got too touchy with him.

I studied the boy in the uniform once more. He wasn't the stereotypical Asian guy. He wasn't short or scrawny, and he didn't wear thick rectangular glasses. No, this boy was *rugged*.

He had short, black hair and flawless pale skin, and a jaw that most guys dreamed of. Even though he was wearing a school uniform, he wore it in a way that made it look less formal. The top two buttons of his white shirt were undone, revealing his strong collarbone, and his black necktie was loosened up. His fingers were hooked on the inner tag of his blazer that hung over his strong shoulder.

Were all of Killian's friends smoking hot?

I looked at Killian and couldn't help but notice how beautiful he looked when he laughed. His head tilted slightly back, and his upper body shook. The corner of his eyes wrinkled from smiling so widely and his bright green eyes shimmered under the sunlight.

Of course, Killian was popular. He was the school's rule-breaker who could knock anyone up with his gaze alone. He was gorgeous, athletic, charming, and he did everything everyone else was too afraid to do. My palms turned clammy just looking at him.

Killian was wearing a white shirt and an unbuttoned vintage flannel with black jeans. I watched him run a hand through his messy, dark hair. Unlike me, he knew how to work the messy bed hair look.

"Psst," Eshe whispered, giving me a gentle nudge. "Stop spacing out."

"I'm not," I lied feebly, quickly looking away from the window. Eshe raised a brow and leaned forward to see what I was looking at. Well, *who* I was looking at.

"Isn't that Killian?" she asked, squinting her eyes.

"Luke's there too," I said.

"How was detention?"

"It was okay."

"Did you talk to Killian?"

"No, not really."

I didn't tell Eshe about our bet. I knew she'd freak out and tell Alix, and I didn't want Alix to worry. Besides, I already knew what they thought of Killian: a bad influence. She thought he was irresponsible, reckless, and an attention seeker. I agreed with the first two, but not the former. Whenever he did something, it was for himself. I envied that.

"Did he bully you?" she asked worriedly.

"No," I mumbled, my voice coming off harsher than I meant. But it irritated me how Alix and Eshe babied me all the time. I could take care of myself. Besides, I already had two suffocating parents at home, I didn't need two more.

She frowned. "Carter—"

"Am I interrupting you two?" our history teacher asked, raising a brow.

"No, sir," we replied sheepishly. Eshe stopped asking questions about Killian, but strangely, I couldn't stop thinking about him.

***

I walked into detention. The classroom was empty as usual, and Mr. Yon was flipping through a new magazine, stuffing his mouth with a handful of chips. He greeted me with a lazy wave, and I took a seat. This time, I sat away from the window, hoping Killian wouldn't sit beside me. Thirty minutes later, the door squeaked open. My chest tightened when I saw Killian step in.

"Killian, you're—"

"Late? I know. I'll be on time tomorrow," Killian said. He didn't even try to sound convincing.

"And I'll win the lottery and become the next president. Take a seat."

These two could be best friends if you forgot about their thirty-year age gap. Killian sat down beside me and greeted me with a warm smile. I felt that strange, giddy feeling again.

"Hey, Jones."

"Why did you come to detention if you didn't come to class?" I mumbled. He looked at me thoughtfully.

"Because I actually enjoy coming to detention."

"Since when?"

"Since I got stuck here with you," he beamed.

There it was again, that strange funny feeling I'd get whenever he was around me.

Look away, look away, look away, a voice in my head screamed at me.

"Don't you ever get tired?" I asked, unable to look away.

"Of?"

"Being bad."

He shrugged casually. "Don't you get tired of being good?"

Touché.

"Anyway, who was the girl you were with the other day? You know, the one who spilled water on Desiree's shoes," he asked.

"Why?" I asked skeptically.

"I'm curious." A pause. "Plus, she's cute."

"She's off-limits," I said defensively, which only made his smile widen. I knew what he was thinking.

"Don't you dare lay a finger on Eshe," I warned him. His brows rose.

"So her name is Eshe," Killian chirped.

Fiddlesticks!

"Are you two dating?" he asked.

"She's my best friend," I clarified coldly.

"So you're both single." Why did I feel like there was an extra adverb in his assumption?

"Yes, but she's not looking for a boyfriend right now."

"I'm probably not her type anyway."

"Not your type?" I echoed.

"Yeah, she seems like the type of girl who likes to settle. Y'know, date one guy, get married, have three kids and whatnot," he said with a wave of a hand. "I'm definitely not her type."

"What do you mean?"

"I'm saying I'm a horny teenager who likes to sleep around," he said shamelessly. "I'm a good friend, the ride or die type of guy. But as a boyfriend? I'm absolute shit. Heck, I wouldn't even date myself."

"Please don't swear," I murmured quietly. He smiled.

"Such a goodie-two-shoes. Speaking of which, I thought about our bet last night and I know what your first dare is going to be."

"What?" I asked nervously.

★* Y.O.L.O - I.J Hidee ★*

"I dare you to ditch detention with me."

"Ditch detention? Mr. Yon will never let us leave."

"Oh, please, he's been asleep since I sat down," Killian said, jerking his thumb towards our P.E teacher who was snoring softly.

"We can't," I repeated. "What if he wakes up? He'll tell Mr. Rodriguez and we'll get in bigger trouble! Do you know what my parents would do to me? And you can't risk getting suspended."

"Aw, are you worried me?" he asked bashfully.

"You're completely missing the point," I groaned.

"You're overthinking. Nothing bad is going to happen."

"A lot of bad things can happen," I argued.

"Come on, don't tell me you're already thinking of quitting. You haven't even got past the first dare."

I didn't answer, looking away.

"Is Carter Jones a quitter?" he gasped.
"I'm not a quitter," I deadpanned.

"I thought you gave it your all when you put your mind to it. I guess I was wrong," he said with a headshake. "But here you are, quitting before even trying," he said dramatically, clutching his chest.

"No, I—"

"A quitter," he moaned in agony. "A quitter who—"

"Alright, fine!" I snapped. "I'll ditch detention with you, but you have to promise that we won't get into any trouble."

A smile etched on his lips.

"I won't let anything happen to you," he said. I found it hard to believe him.

He grabbed his bag and headed for the door. I quickly gathered my things and followed him. I stopped and glanced at Mr. Yon who twitched and scratched his unshaven beard. The scratchy noise made me shiver.

Killian gestured for me to hurry up and I quickly walked past the front desk. I stopped at the threshold. My hands tightened at my sides as I stared at the silver line. Was I really going to ditch detention? Once I stepped out of here, there was no turning back.

I pursed my lips.

This is a bad idea. What am I thinking?

But then I remembered what Killian said.

"Aren't you Carter Jones? The one who hardly has any friends, spends his free time studying, and who follows every rule that exists including the rules that probably don't?"

I pressed my lips together as his words hammered into my brain.

★* Y.O.L.O - I.J Hidee ★*

"You live a safe but boring life."

My jaw tightened.

"You're too chicken to do anything outside your comfort zone."

"Are you coming?" Killian asked, snapping me out of my thoughts. I took in a tight breath, stepping over the line. I did it. I actually did it. And for some reason, I didn't hate it. It felt kind of thrilling. Exciting even.

Was I going to regret this? Sure. Was I going to feel guilty? Definitely. But Y.O.L.O, right?

"Atta boy," Killian grinned, putting his arm around my shoulder and pulling me closer towards him as we walked down the corridors. I don't think he knew how hyperaware I became when he touched me.

While I tried not to blush, he didn't even seem to notice the proximity between us.

"Where are we going?" I asked nervously, tightening my grip around the straps of my bag. When I looked up, he smiled at me, his green eyes glistening with mischief.

"Somewhere fun."

Chapter 7: Playing Dirty

We've been walking for fifteen minutes, and I still didn't know where we were going. I anxiously looked around us, scared that a teacher might see us.

"Will you relax?" Killian chuckled.

"I am relaxed," I said.

"You've been looking over your shoulder like a serial killer is stalking us."

I stiffened. "Where are we going?"

"You know you don't have to whisper," he said, which was when I noticed how small my voice was. I cleared my throat.

"Right," I said a little louder.

"We're almost there, don't worry."

To my surprise, we went into a mall. Were we going shopping? But we walked past the clothes stores and took the escalator to the third floor. Killian headed towards the area with flashing lights and loud music.

"The arcade?" I asked. I've never been to the arcade. Sure, I've walked past it, but I've never been inside of it. My parents told me that games were a waste of time and space.

"I told you I'd take you somewhere fun," he grinned.

"I like quiet places where I can read books and do useful things," I replied bluntly. Killian scowled.

"What are you, an old man?"

"Games are bad for the eyes and can affect our brains. I read an article—"

"Right, lecture me later, old man," he said, entering the arcade without letting me finish.

I stood outside and looked over my shoulder, scared that Mr. Yon might pop out of nowhere and hit me with his magazine to shoo away my sins. I shook my head at the disturbing thought and jogged to catch up with my partner in crime.

"Killian!" But the music was too loud for him to hear me. I had to tug on his sleeve to get his attention.

"I didn't bring any money," I said.

"Don't worry, I got you."

Before I could protest, he told me to wait here. He went to the front desk to buy some coins but ended up flirting with the pretty employee working behind the desk.

Unbelievable.

I studied Killian from head to toe. He was tall and had broad shoulders, and he had a firm butt and strong legs. You could tell that he worked out. Some of the girls in the arcade glanced at him and nudged at their friends to look his way. He seemed to have a natural aura that attracted people wherever he went. Maybe I should start working out too.

Who was I kidding? I couldn't even do a single push-up.

There was a mirror in front of me and I turned to the side to look at my bum.

Maybe if I start doing squats my thighs will be as sturdy as Killian's.

"Are you checking yourself out?"

I jumped in surprise. Killian stood in front of me with a bowl of silver coins. He slipped his phone into his pocket.

"Did you get the girl's number?" I asked.

"What do you take me for?" he asked defensively. Before I could apologize, he smiled with a wink. "Of course, I got her number."

"Right," I grumbled.

"Let's throw some hoops," he said, heading to the basketball machines. He gave me two silver coins. I studied the machine, trying to find out where to insert them.

"Over there," Killian said. His fingers brushed over mine when he took the coins from my hand. He inserted them into the slot for me and the machine came to life. He put some coins in his machine and mini basketballs came rolling out. He threw one and it went in. He glanced at me, tilting his head with a lopsided grin.

"You should hurry if you want to win," he chuckled. I tossed one towards the net but stopped when I heard Killian bark into laughter.

"You're supposed to throw the balls at your net, not mine," he said. "You just scored two points for me."

My eyes widened in embarrassment.

"Right, I knew that."

We started playing. This time, I shot at my net. I glanced at his score.

55?! I was still at 4!

I checked the timer. We only had one minute left. I panicked and decided to play dirty, stealing his basketballs while trying to distract him. I tried to push his rock-hard body away, but he wouldn't budge.

"What are you doing?" he asked as I jumped up and down in front of him like a bunny to stop him from shooting.

"Two can play dirty," he smirked. He wrapped his strong arms around my legs and threw me over his shoulder like I weighed nothing. I yelped when I rose from the ground, grabbing onto him so I wouldn't fall over.
"Put me down!" I cried, banging my small fists against his back which obviously didn't affect him one bit because I could hear his score going up.

"Alright, alright, I'm sorry!" I huffed in defeat, but the game ended. I looked over my shoulder, my eyes widening at his score.

72?! I sighed in defeat.

"Okay, you win. Now can you put me down?" I sulked. He chuckled, patting my bum before setting me back on my feet.

"Four isn't bad for a beginner," he said with a smug smile.

"Shoo," I mumbled, swatting him away. Killian started putting in another coin and my brows pulled together. "What are you doing?"

"Giving you another chance. Here, I'll help you this time," he said. Hesitant at first, I picked up a basketball and threw it at the net. We watched it fly over the machine and disappear to who knows where. I blinked blankly while Killian laughed so hard, he almost fell to the floor.

An employee appeared and handed me the basketball, asking me not to do that again before leaving with a strange look on his face.

Killian was still laughing.

"I don't want to play if you're going to keep making fun of me."

"Sorry, you're just too cute," he chuckled, wiping away his tears. My face reddened and I looked away, feeling my heart race inside my chest. He's probably said that to a million other girls.

"Here, I'll teach you how to shoot." Killian pulled me towards him and pressed my back against his broad chest. I held my breath. Weren't we standing too close? I gulped at how hard and sculpted he felt.

"The trick is to bend your knees," he murmured, his husky sending shivers down my spine. "Put your right hand like this, and your hand left slightly under."

He helped me position them around the ball. "You good?"

My knees buckled and I gulped with a nod.

"Keep your eyes on the net and pretend like you're aiming for the front part of the hoop," he instructed. I bit my lower lip, trying my best to focus on the hoop instead of Killian. I took in a deep breath and tossed the ball. My eyes widened when it went in.

"We did it!" I exclaimed, jumping up and down in excitement. We high-fived and our fingers intertwined. "It actually went in!"

"Congratulation, Jones," he smiled warmly. I noticed we were still holding hands and quickly pulled away.

"Sorry," I apologized.

"Let's try another game," he said, heading to the other machines. I was about to follow him but froze. Why was I smiling so widely? Was I actually enjoying myself? And with Killian? I looked up at him, but the smile on my face wouldn't go away.

"Killian, wait for me!"

★* Y.O.L.O - I.J Hidee ★*

Chapter 8: Bad Boy Jones

We spent the afternoon playing in the arcade. I don't think I've ever had that much fun in my life. I almost forgot that we were supposed to be in detention.

"We still have two coins left," Killian said, fishing out the remaining coins. "What do you want to do before we leave?"

My eyes gravitated towards a machine at the back of the arcade. Killian followed my gaze.

"You wanna try the claw machine?" he asked. I quickly looked away.

"We can do something else," I said. Killian didn't look like the type of guy who'd play the claw machine. I looked around to find something that might fit his taste.

"We can play the zombie apocalypse game if you want."

Why would you suggest that, Carter? You're terrified of zombies!

"No way, the claw machine is a classic."

I had a feeling he was saying that for my sake.

"Come on, let's go," he said. I squeezed my hands together, trying to hide my excitement. My eyes brightened when I saw the pile of cute stuffed animals caged behind a glass wall. I wanted to save all of them.

"You were looking at this one, right?" Killian said, nodding his chin towards the machine with the stuffed teddy bears.

"Yeah," I admitted sheepishly. "But this game is wack. You never get the prizes inside."

He inserted a coin and patted the machine.

"Give it a go. You probably wouldn't win even if they weren't wack," he winked. My jaw dropped and I narrowed my eyes at him. Challenge accepted. I pulled up my sleeves, all fired up.

"I'll show you," I growled.

"Please," he smiled brightly.

I shifted the stick and moved the claw towards the brown teddy bear at the top of the pile. When it was right above it, I pressed the red button and anxiously watched the metal claw lower towards the prize. It grabbed the teddy bear by the ear, and I gasped when it picked it up, but right before it reached the hole, the teddy bear slipped from the claw and fell back into the pile.

"I failed," I frowned.

"Not yet."

★* Y.O.L.O - I.J Hidee ★*

Killian inserted another coin and put his hand over mine. His face was so close to mine. He shifted the stick and pressed the red button. I leaned closer towards the glass, watching the claw scoop up a teddy bear.

Almost there, almost there, almost there...

A gasped when the teddy bear fell into the hole. Killian crouched down and took it out of the slot.

"And you said this game was wack," he grinned in self-satisfaction.

"You did it!" I exclaimed.

"*We* did it," he said. "Here, it's yours."

"Really?"

"You seem to like it more than I do."

I couldn't stop smiling. This had to be the best day ever. I took the teddy bear with both hands and hugged it tightly against my chest. It was so soft and fluffy. Panda was going to love his new friend.

"Thank you, Killian. You're the best!"

Killian's eyes widened, then he quickly looked away.

"What's wrong? Are you okay?" I asked, tilting my head to see his face.

"We should get going. It's getting late," he said briefly. He walked away, but I noticed that his ears were slightly pink.

No, I was probably imagining things.

We left the mall and Killian placed a cigarette between his lips. He lit the tip like he's done it a thousand times before and inhaled, blowing the smoke through the corner of his lips so it wouldn't come my way.

"Why do you smoke?" I frowned.

"It helps calm my stress and bitter thoughts," he answered, flicking the ashes with a thoughtful look on his face. "Life's been tough since my dad left."

"Oh," I frowned. "I'm so—"

A teasing smile grew on his lips and his green eyes flickered towards me.

"You expected me to say something like that, didn't you?" he smirked. I paused.

"Wait, that was a lie?" I asked in disbelief.

"Partially. I smoke 'cause I like the feeling."

"That *feeling* is slowly killing you," I frowned.

"Better die young and happy than old with regrets," he shrugged. I pursed my lips, hesitant at first.

"Can I try one?"

Killian raised his eyebrows in surprise. I knew how bad smoking was. I've watched documentaries on it and read books about lung cancer, but I was curious. It was something I wanted to try at least once in my life.

"Did Carter Jones just ask me for a cigarette?"

"I just want to know what it feels like." I squirmed when he stared at me. "Never mind, forget that I asked."

"Here," he said, handing me a cigarette. "I don't think you'll like it anyway."

"Will I die?"

"I promise you won't," he laughed.

"What do I do with it?"

"You hold it between your index and middle finger and place it between your lips," he said, showing me how to do it. I followed his instructions and he handed me his lighter. I put my thumb on the metal spark wheel but stopped.

"What's wrong?" he asked.

"I'm scared. Can you do it for me?"

I was scared I'd burn my thumb.

"'Course," he grunted. Killian took the lighter and rolled down the spark wheel with the pad of his thumb. A flame flickered then vanished. He shook the lighter and tried again, but only a small spark came out.

"Huh, I guess I'm all out," he mumbled, trying again with no success.

"Maybe this is a sign from the universe telling me not to smoke," I murmured, trying to hide my disappointment.

"Well, screw the universe," he smirked.

He put his hand on the back of my neck and lowered his head to my height, gently pulling me towards him. The tip of his cigarette was now touching mine. Our eyes locked and I could feel myself getting lost in his green hues, my heart racing against my chest as my cheeks started to blush.

"Suck," he ordered, his cigarette still perched between his lips. I did as I was told and the fire from his cigarette caught onto mine. Smoke filled my mouth.

"Now swallow," he ordered softly. I tried, but the bitter taste got caught in my throat and I pulled away, coughing and gagging.

"It's so bitter!" I hissed.

"I told you you wouldn't like it."

He took the cigarette and pressed the bud against the outdoor ashtray. I scrunched my face and stuck my tongue out. No wonder this stuff kills people. My eyes widened when I had a lightbulb moment.

"I know what your first dare is going to be!" I gasped, swiveling my head towards Killian. He had an uneasy look on his face.
"What?"

"You have to give up smoking until our bet is over."

He stared at me as if I was crazy, then tried to laugh it off.

"You're kidding, right?"

I stretched out my hand and motioned for him to give me his cigarettes.

"Come on, big boy, hand them over."

His smile dropped. "I won't survive a day without them."

"Do you hear that?"

"Hear what?" His eyes then widened. "Jones, don't you dare—"

"Bawk," I clucked. "Bacawk."

"Jones," he warned me.

"What's that, buckawk?"

"Stop—"

"Bok bok."

"Jones," he groaned.

"Buck, buck, bacawk," I went on, hopping on one foot and then the other with my hands on my hips, looking like a complete fool. "Mooo—" Oh snap, wrong animal. "I mean bok bok."

Killian tossed me his cigarettes which I barely managed to catch.

"Fine, I'll give up the cigs, just please stop with that unbearable chicken noises."

I slipped the cigarettes into my pocket.

"It's for your own good," I told him.

"But terrible for my sanity," he mumbled under his breath. "Take care of my babies, alright?"

His phone rang.

"You mind?" he asked.

I shook my head. "No, go ahead."

He nodded and walked a few meters away before answering. I heard a few 'mhm's,' and 'yeah's,' and then a 'tonight?' A pause.

"Alright, I'll see you later," he said, hanging up. He looked over at me. "Sorry, Jones, seems like our date is going to have to end here."

Date?

"Where are you going?" Why did I sound so sad?

"Booty call," he winked.
My voice fell to a whisper. "Oh."

"Why don't you give me your number?"

"Why?" I asked, confused.

★* Y.O.L.O - I.J Hidee ★*

"So I can text you when I miss you, silly."

"How many times have you used that one?" I snorted.

"It's actually my first."

I couldn't tell if he was joking or not, but I gave him my number.

"I hardly use my phone though," I frowned.

"I can change that," he said confidently. "I'll see you around, Jones. I had fun today."

I watched him disappear around the corner, and pressed my lips together.

"I had fun too."

★* Y.O.L.O - I.J Hidee ★*

Chapter 9: Therapy with Kiwi

I came to school the next day with terrible bags under my eyes. I hardly got a wink of sleep, not after committing such a big crime yesterday. I didn't know whether I felt guilty for ditching detention or guilty for actually enjoying it.

Killian was right. Mr. Yon didn't contact our parents or the principal. Nobody knew that we had ditched detention except us. That was another thing I couldn't stop thinking about. Killian. I had so much fun at the arcade with him; it was unforgettable.

'You're just too cute.'

His voice echoed inside my mind for the hundredth time. I groaned, pressing my forehead against the table. The students in the library turned around and hushed me.

"Sorry," I mumbled, too tired to sound genuine.

"What's wrong?" Eshe whispered.

"Nothing," I lied. I also felt guilty for not telling my best friend about the bet.

"Something's obviously on your mind."

When I didn't answer, she said, "Are you still bummed about detention?"

"Oh, uh, yeah," I mumbled.

"Do you want me to sneak into the detention for you?"

"No!" I blurted.

"It's fine. I won't get into any trouble. What is the principal going to do? Punish me for sneaking into detention?" she chuckled. "We can study and do our homework together."

"It's okay, you don't have to do that for me," I told her. I didn't want Eshe to come to detention, but not for the same reason as she probably thought. She raised her brows at my hostility.

"O-kay," she said. We heard high heels nearby and I looked over my shoulder.

Desiree and her two best friends walked into the library wearing matching pink outfits and deadly heels that looked like weapons more than shoes. None of their outfits followed the dress code, but Desiree didn't seem to care. And when the queen B didn't care, neither did her friends.

Desiree eyes stopped on Eshe, and a look of pure disgust spread across her face.
"Something smells rotten," Desiree said, waving her hand in front of her nose. Her friends giggled.

"Yeah, take a shower," Eshe snorted. Desiree's mouth fell ajar.

"I was talking about you."

"Nah, I'm pretty sure it's you."

Desiree rolled her eyes and made a dramatic walk out of the library. When she was gone, Eshe groaned.

"Ugh, I can't stand her," Eshe muttered. "How do people even like her?"

"At least she notices you," I teased. Desiree didn't even spare me a glance. She rarely paid attention to anyone who didn't have the same social status as her, so it surprised me that Eshe was even in her radar.

It also surprised me that Eshe let her get under her skin. She normally ignored people like Desiree and didn't care what they said, but the girls seemed to mutually despise each other.

"Whatever," Eshe said. She didn't seem to want to talk about Desiree, so I changed the subject.

"Can you help me finish this equation?"

She scooted her chair closer to mine. I thought I'd feel my heart race and my stomach twist, the same way it did whenever Killian was close to me, but I didn't feel anything.

"Carter?"

I looked up from the paper and stared at Eshe who now looked annoyed. I hadn't been paying attention at all.

"Sorry," I apologized. "I need some fresh air."

I briskly stood up, but something fell out of my pockets. Before I could reach for it, Eshe picked it up first.

"Are these cigarettes?" she asked in shock.

"Shhhh," hushed the other students.

"Oh, don't hush me," she snapped back before snapping her head towards me.

"I can explain," I stammered.

"Since when do you smoke?"

"I don't!"

She waved the cigarettes in front of me. "Then explain this!"

She raised her voice, so I pulled her out of the library before the librarian kicked us out. She pulled away from me and stopped, crossing her arms over her chest while stabbing me with a death glare.

"Explain," she ordered coldly.

"I don't smoke," I said, then paused. "Okay, I tried one cigarette."
"You what?!"

"I saw Killian smoking and wanted to try one too."

She jerked her head back.

"Wait, what?"

This wasn't going the way I had hoped. I nervously fiddled with my sleeves, trying to think of something to say. I didn't want to tell Eshe about the bet I made with Killian or the fact that I ditched detention with him. I had no other choice but to lie.

"One, I smoked one cigarette. No, I didn't even smoke half of it. I was curious, that's all. I won't do it again, I promise."

Eshe studied my face then sighed.

"You know how bad smoking is for your health," she murmured softly.

"Yeah, I know," I said quietly. Eshe was holding the cigarettes, but Killian told me to take good care of his babies. "Can I have them back? I need to return them to Killian."

"I don't trust him."

"Alix said the same thing," I chuckled half-heartedly.

"He's right. Killian isn't like us."

"What do you mean?" I asked.
"We're the good kids, the nerds of the school. We get straight A's, we don't miss a day of school, we don't break curfew. Killian? He's a troublemaker."

I frowned.

"He's a bad influence, and you'll end up getting hurt if you get too close to him. Water doesn't mix with oil; it just doesn't happen."

Her words stung, but I couldn't argue with her.

"Just don't forget who you are," she murmured, handing me the cigarettes. She went back into the library, and I was left alone in the halls.

She was right. I was Carter Jones, the good boy who stayed away from the bad. That was the way things were, and that was the way things were going to be.

…Right?

***

I was in detention, anxiously fiddling with my pen. I constantly glanced at my watch, waiting for the minute hand to strike thirty. But Killian never came. Detention felt empty without him, and I went home, disappointed and sad.

Without him, my life fell back to its normal monotonous routine. He was the gravy to my potatoes; the one person who added flavor to my boring life.
I got home, took a shower, had dinner with my parents, answered their predictable questions, and went up to my room to study. My phone buzzed. An unknown caller was calling me. It was Killian. It had to be him.

I wanted to pick up and ask him why he didn't come to detention, but I decided not to answer. I wasn't allowed to answer phone calls. The only exception I made was for Alix. Besides, Eshe was probably right. Having expectations and hopes for someone who didn't like commitment or responsibilities was an open gateway to getting hurt.

Killian didn't show up for detention the next day. I was starting to get worried. Did something happen to him? Maybe I should have answered his call last night.

After dinner, I finished my homework and read a book. I flipped to the next page but realized that my mind wasn't processing any of the words, so I had to constantly flip back to re-read the pages. I sighed in frustration, tilting my head back. All I could think about was Killian.

I picked up Kiwi, the teddy bear Killian gave me at the arcade. I sat him on my lap and stared into his beady black eyes.

"What do you think I should do?" I asked. "Do you think Killian is a bad guy and that I should stay away from him?"

I poked Kiwi's furry belly.

If Killian was a bad guy, then he wouldn't have helped you get the soda out of the vending machine, I imagined Kiwi say. *If he was really a bad person, then he wouldn't have dumped a plate of spaghetti on Desiree's head for you. He even took you to the arcade and gave me to you.*

"But everyone around me keeps telling me that he's a bad influence," I frowned.

Are you going to spend the rest of your life listening to what others think? What about you? What do you think about him?

"I've never seen anyone like him. He does what he wants, makes his own decision, and lives life to the fullest. I admire him because he does everything I'm too scared to do."

I stared at Kiwi and my head fell.

"I must be losing my mind," I muttered, tossing Kiwi aside in frustration. I sat there, pursed my lips, then quickly picked him back up and hugged him against my chest.

"I'm sorry, Kiwi, I didn't mean to hurt you," I said, planting a gentle kiss on his head. I carefully put him beside Panda and lied down beside them.

Yeah, I must really be going crazy.

Chapter 10: A Strange Feeling

I was about to fall asleep when my phone rang. It was the same unknown number as the other day. This time, I answered.

"Hello?"

"Finally." When I recognized Killian's voice, my heart did a little backflip. "I thought you gave me a fake phone number or something."

"I told you that I don't use my phone a lot."

"And I told you I'd change that." I could hear the smile in his voice. I wrapped my arms around Kiwi, secretly happy.

"You didn't come to detention," I murmured quietly.

"My best friend got into some trouble."

"Luke?" I asked.

"Nah, Francisco."

Was he the boy wearing the school uniform?

"What happened?"

"I had to help him get away from the police."

"You what?!"

"Long story," he chuckled, then his voice was serious. "Don't worry, no one died."

That did not reassure me one bit. You didn't put 'don't worry' and 'die' in the same sentence.

"Anyway, how have you been?"

"I've been okay. Why did you call?"

"I wanted to check up on you."

"Oh." A pause. "Okay, I'll hang up now."

"Wait!" he blurted. He sighed with a shaky laugh. "Honestly, Jones, you can be so blunt sometimes. Since we're on the phone, we might as well talk."

I nibbled on my lower lip. I guess it wouldn't hurt to talk a bit.

"Can I ask you something?" I asked.

"Shoot."

"Are you gay?"

"What?" he coughed.

"Do you like guys?"

"Yeah, I understood you the first time. I just wasn't expecting it," he said. "Why do you ask?"

I nibbled on my lower lip. "Never mind, forget that I asked."

"You can't say never mind after asking me such a scandalous question," he chuckled. I hesitated at first.

"There's been a rumor going around in school saying that you were caught sucking another boy in the boy's locker room."

I jumped when Killian burst into laughter.

"Are people still spreading around such nonsense? Jones, if every rumor at school was true, then I'd have two dicks and four nipples."

Oh, so I guess he wasn't—

"As if I'd suck off another guy's dick," he snorted as if it was the most ridiculous thing he's heard. "He'd be sucking mine."

My eyes widened at how straightforward *he* was. He didn't sound embarrassed at all. I decided to quickly change the subject.

"Killian?"

"Mhm?"

"Can I ask you another question?"

"Well, isn't someone curious today," he mused. "Maybe I should ditch detention more often."

"No!" I blurted. "I... I like it when you come."

There was a short silence that followed. Did he hang up?

"Your question," Killian grunted, his voice a little huskier.

"Why did you dump the plate of spaghetti on Desiree's head? You didn't know me or Eshe, so I thought it was weird that you helped us out."

"I kind of knew who you were."

My eyes fluttered in surprise.

"Weren't you always crying behind the bushes in front of the school gates?"

"You saw that?!" I asked in horror.

"Yeah, I used to smoke near there."

My heart dropped and I dug my face against my pillow in embarrassment. I couldn't believe that Killian saw me crying. I thought no one would be there.

"Why did you cry?" Killian asked softly. It took me a moment to reply.

"I get stressed a lot," I murmured. "From school and my parents."

"Do they know?"

★* Y.O.L.O - I.J Hidee ★*

My voice was quiet. "No."

I flinched when he let out a heavy sigh.

"I know you want to make them proud, but is it really worth sacrificing your happiness?"

The tone of his voice caught me by surprise.

"Why are you wasting your time trying to please others? One day, you're going to die, so why waste your life trying to be what others expect you to be? You're young. Do what you want, say what you want, and don't let others tell you otherwise. Stop waiting for a stupid diploma to define who you are, or a dumb job that you won't even like. Live now and take risks. This is your life, not theirs."

Killian, a boy who've I've only known for only a week, made me question my entire life.

"I guess that's why I wanted to make a bet with you," he murmured.

"What do you mean?"

"Well, I'm the opposite of you. I've been living life without rules, but I feel like I'm getting lost in my own abuse of freedom. Everything feels the same, like life has become a boring routine. I thought that maybe someone like you, someone opposite from me, could help me find what living once really means," he said. "Maybe we can help each other out."

I nodded with a small smile. "I hope we do."

★* Y.O.L.O - I.J Hidee ★*

My phone rang. It was Eshe's older sister, Anna. She wouldn't call me if it wasn't something important.

"Just a sec," I said, putting Killian on hold. "Anna?"

"Pumpkin ran away!" she yelled.

My eyebrows drew together. "Again?"

"I opened the window and she just jumped out. I've looked everywhere but I can't find her. My parents went to pick up Eshe and they won't be back until another hour. They're going to *kill* me if they find out that I lost our cat again."

"I'm sure Pumpkin didn't go too far. She never does."

"Can you help me find her? Please?"

I pursed my lips, but Anna sounded really stressed. "Okay, I'll go."

"Thank you, thank you, thank you," she gushed. "I'll meet you at the city park. She normally hides in the forest."

She hung up and I was back on the line with Killian.

"I have to go help my friend find Pumpkin."

"Pumpkin?" he asked, confused. I laughed nervously.
"Yeah, her cat. She's an orange Tangee cat," I explained. "It was either that or Garfield."

People thought she got her name from the color of her fur, but they actually named her Pumpkin because she looked like one.

"Do you want me to help look for her?" Killian asked.

"I don't want to trouble you," I frowned.

"It's fine, I'll get to see you," he said with a smile in his voice. "Where should we meet?"

I bit my lower lip. "The city park."

"Alright, I'll see you there."

He hung up and I plopped onto my bed, staring at the ceiling with my hand over my racing chest.

Why did I feel this way?

★* Y.O.L.O - I.J Hidee ★*

Chapter 11: I Feel Ugly

Killian and I made it to the park at the same time. Anna was already there when we arrived.

"Hey, Anna!" I called, jogging up to her.

"Carter, I'm so glad you're—" she stopped when she saw Killian. "Well, helloooo there, hubba bubba."

"Hi, I'm Killian," he smiled, extending a hand. "I probably have class with your sister, but I wouldn't know."

Anna giggled and snorted, shaking Killian's hand in a dainty way.

"Hi, Killian," she said dreamily, batting her long lashes. "I'm Anna, Eshe's hot, older, *single* sister."

She emphasized the single and I tried not to groan. Killian simply smiled. I noticed that they were still holding hands. Well, that Anna was holding Killian's hand. I cleared my voice.

"We should look for Pumpkin," I said.

"Oh, right," Anna said, pulling away and almost sounding disappointed. "Here, I brought you a flashlight. I know you're scared of the dark."

My eyes darted to Killian whose smile widened. Yeah, he definitely heard.

"You're scared of the dark?" he mused.

"No," I said, but my voice cracked. I felt myself slowly dying inside. I tried to play it cool and said, "It's just that I like it better when the sun is out and when I can see what's in front of me. It's a preference, not a fear."

Anna rolled her eyes. "He's a total scaredy cat," she smirked.

"Anna!" I cried.

"You should try watching a horror movie with him. He'll stick to you like glue."

My mouth fell open at her betrayal.

"I'll keep that in mind," Killian chuckled, the mischievous glimmer in his eyes making me stiffen.

"Pumpkin," I reminded them, eager to change the subject.

"You're right, let's go," Anna said. We walked into the forest. Killian's arm brushed against mine as he lowered his head to my height.

"Scaredy cat Jones. Sounds catchy, don't you think?" he teased.

"Leave me alone," I grumbled, pushing him away.

We went deeper into the forest. Killian and Anna chatted like they've known each other for years. I could hear them cracking jokes behind me. I felt left out and was slightly jealous.

Wait, what was I saying? Why would I be jealous?

A sudden rustling noise caught my attention. It got louder and louder.

"Guys, I think—" but when I turned around, I noticed that the noise wasn't coming from Pumpkin, but from Killian and Anna. They were unwrapping their lollipops. I gaped at them in disbelief, and they looked up at me, clueless.

"Oh, sorry, did you want one?" Killian asked, offering me his. I twitched.

"I'm good," I grumbled, turning on my heel and marching forward.

We heard a 'meow' coming from above. Killian raised his phone and the beam of light reflected two beady red eyes.

"Pumpkin!" Anna exclaimed, raising her hands in the air as if to greet God. "Come here, Pumpkin, come to mama."

She started making weird kissing noises that cat people made to get Pumpkin's attention but was ignored completely.

"I like her," Killian grunted.

"What should we do? The branch is too high," she frowned.

"One of us can lift another up," I suggested.

"Who's the strongest?" Anna asked. Without question, we simultaneously turned towards Killian. "And who's the shortest?"

I looked at Anna, but Anna and Killian turned towards me.

"I'm a few inches taller than you," I said to Anna, putting my back against hers to prove it. I sucked in as much air as I could and raised my chin. "Killian, who's taller?" I winced.

"Anna."

My jaw dropped open and Anna giggled.

"Oh, but if you're too scared to go up, I'll happily volunteer. Killian, why don't you lift me up—"

"Come on, Jones, we have a cat to save," he said, walking towards me. Before I could stop him, he crouched down and wrapped his arms around my calves. I squeaked when he lifted me off the ground and grabbed onto his shoulders.

"Am I heavy?" I asked worriedly.

"Light as a feather," he promised. "Can you reach the branch?"

I stretched my arms up and wrapped my fingers around the branch.

"Yeah, I got it," I said.

"Can you pull yourself up?"

I looked down at him with a sheepish look.

"Um..."

He released me and I yelped, my feet dangling in the air. I tried to pull myself up. No success. I could feel my fingers slipping from the branch.

"Killian!" I cried in panic.

He came to my rescue and lowered me to the ground. I looked at my palms and frowned at the scratches and bark marks.

"Ouch," I pouted.

"Let me see," Killian said, but I hid my hands behind my back and shook my head.

"I'm fine," I said.

He took my hands anyway and uncurled my fingers. We were once again standing close to each other, his face only a few inches away from mine. Gosh, how could he be so handsome? He studied my injuries with a frown.

"Does it hurt?" he asked sternly, his voice low and thick.

"No, I'm okay," I whispered, surprised by how big his hands were compared to mine. But Killian didn't look convinced. "Really, I'm okay."

"Um, guys?" Anna coughed. "The cat?"

I pulled away from Killian, feeling my face redden.

"Should I try again?" I asked.

"No," Killian said.

He handed me his phone before jumping up and grabbing the lowest branch. Anna and I watched with wide eyes as he swiftly pulled himself up. He reached Pumpkin in just a few seconds and climbed back down. His phone buzzed, and I looked down at the screen.

56 unread messages?! Just how popular was he?!

I didn't mean to look, but I read the first message.

Amber: Are you really going to break up with me after last night? And through text?!

Killian handed Anna her cat and I quickly turned off the screen.

"Where did you learn how to do that?" She asked in awe. "Do you work out?"

She gently squeezed Killian's biceps and giggled.

"Oh, you definitely work out. You know, I just so happen to go to the gym too. If you're free, maybe we can—"

"Home," I blurted. They turned towards me, and I briskly walked past them, making sure to cut in between them. "We should go home now."

"Hey, wait up!" Anna called.

What was with this ugly feeling that I got when Anna stood too close to Killian? Or when he received a text from another girl? I couldn't be jealous, could I? I mean, why would I? It wasn't like I had feelings for him.

My eyes stretched open and I felt the blood in my face drain down my neck.

I couldn't be catching feelings for Killian, could I?

We were almost out of the forest. I shoved my hands into my pockets and stiffened, frantically patting them. They were empty.

"What's wrong?" Anna asked, but I was already running back into the forest.

"Where are you going?" Killian called.

"You guys go on without me! I think I left something behind."

Killian shouted something, but he was too far for me to hear.

★* Y.O.L.O - I.J Hidee ★*

Chapter 12: Hold My Hand Little Teapot

I frantically look around, trying to find the tree that Pumpkin was sitting on. My eyes widened when my flashlight reflected something shiny. I quickly ran towards it and smiled in triumph, picking up Killian's cigarette packet, the one that I had dropped. I never thought that I'd be so happy to see a cigarette packet with the words 'Smoking Kills' above a picture of rotting, dark lungs.

"Thank goodness," I sighed to myself, but I stiffened when I realized that I was alone. The wind made a spooky ghost-like noise and I shivered. I really didn't think things through, did I?

"Everything is going to be okay," I said to myself.

My flashlight died and I was immediately consumed in darkness. I tried to turn the flashlight back on, hitting it against my palm, but only a few flickers came out. I even took out the batteries and bit the middle before putting it back in, but the batteries were dead.

I took in a deep breath.

"Just go back the way you came, Carter. Look straight ahead and don't look back."

I started walking and tried to distract myself by singing a cheerful song.

"I'm a little teapot, short and stout," I stammered. "Here is my handle, here is my spout." I forgot the rest of the lyrics, so I improvised. "Something, something, something, lalala…"

The bushes behind me rustled and I yelped, crouching down, and putting my arms over my head. A twig cracked and I heard something approach me. Was it a bear?

"Please don't hurt me," I begged. "I don't taste very good, I promise!"

"I'm not going to hurt you," the bear replied. Wait, since when did bears talk?

I opened my watery eyes. Killian looked at me with worried and confused eyes. Before he could say anything, I leaped forward and wrapped my arms around him. My clammy hands clutched onto his shirt, and I dug my face into his shoulder, my entire body shaking with fear.

He was here. He was really here.

"Jones, are you okay?" Killian asked. I nodded when I obviously wasn't.

"Why did you run into the forest by yourself?"

"I thought I lost your cigarettes."

There was a pause. Was he mad?

"Hey," he murmured, cupping my face in his hands. "Did you really run back just to find my cigarettes?"

I nodded, feeling embarrassed and pathetic. My gaze fell to his chest and my voice came out as a small whisper.

"You told me to take care of your babies."

"Oh, Jones," he laughed softly. "I could have just bought another packet."

My lower lip quivered, and I punched his chest. Well, calling it a punch was an overstatement. I think I hurt myself more than I hurt him, but he played along for my sake.

"Ouch," he said, rubbing his left pec.

"Can't you tell me that I did a good job? I ran all the way here to find your cigarettes and… and…"

But I was interrupted by a small gasp, the unexpected ones that came out when you cried. I burst into tears. He laughed, hugging my head against his chest.

"Thank you for taking care of my babies," he whispered into my hair.

"You're welcome," I sobbed, ugly crying. He held onto me until I calmed down.

"As much as I'd like to keep hugging you, it's getting late. Can you get up?" he asked. I nodded, but he helped me on my feet anyway and brushed away the dirt on my pants. He turned to leave, but I quickly reached out and held onto his sleeve. He looked over his shoulder, confused.

"So we don't lose each other," I explained, scared that Killian might yell Y.O.L.O before prancing away and leaving me behind.

"You're going to stretch my clothes if you hold me like that. Why don't you hold my hand instead?"

"My hands are sweaty," I said nervously. I was insecure about my clammy hands. What if he thought it was disgusting?

"I don't mind."

But I didn't budge.

"Alright then. For your second dare, I want you to hold my hand," Killian said. My brows quirked in surprise.

"You're going to waste a dare on that?" I frowned.

He shrugged. "The whole point of the bet is to get you out of your comfort zone. It's not really a waste. Besides, it's a win-win if you ask me."

A win-win?

Hesitant at first, I finally took his hand. I thought he would pull away or grimace when he felt my clammy palms, but he didn't seem bothered at all. He gave me a gentle squeeze instead.

"Since you gave me my second dare, can I give you yours?" I asked as we started walking.

"Sure."

"We have a science test next week and I want you to take the test."

Next week's test counted for 40% of our final grade. If Killian didn't take the test, he'd fail his school year.

"I don't like studying," he mumbled. "Sitting on a chair and staring at books stresses me out."

"It's our responsibility as teenagers to go to school and take tests."

"Responsibilities. Going to school. Taking... Tests," he shivered.

I raised my eyebrows.

"So I guess I win the bet?"

"Wow, hold on, no one's won the bet yet. You really want me to take the test?"

I nodded. He sighed, raking a hand through his hair.

"How am I supposed to say no when you're looking at me like that? Alright, I'll accept your dare."

We made it to the city part. Time seemed to fly whenever I was with him.

"How far do you live?" he asked me.

"About fifteen minutes away."

"I'll walk you home."

"No, it's fine," I quickly said. "It's late and you've already helped me enough."

"It's fine, I had fun. Besides, I'll worry if you walk home by yourself."

"Are you sure you don't mind?" I frowned.

"Positive," he smiled, and he didn't let go of my hand the entire way home.

★* Y.O.L.O - I.J Hidee ★*

Chapter 13: How Do I Reverse This Feeling?

I let out a small groan as I felt a warm ray of sunlight on my face, pulling the covers over my head to hide in the dark.

Wait.

My eyes flung open, and I looked at my clock.

7:45 a.m?!

I jumped out of bed, brushed my teeth, splashed water on my face, and changed into a fresh pair of clothes. When I got home, I was so exhausted that I had forgotten to set my alarm.

I grabbed my bike from the shed and was about to pedal away but stopped. I threw my bike on the grass and dashed into the house to grab my bright red helmet. I adjusted it on my head and gave it a lucky pat.

When I arrived at school, I had two minutes before class started. My eyes widened when I saw Killian walking down the other side of the hall. He looked just as surprised as I was.

"Hey, Jones. Trying to run a marathon?" he smiled. His pearly white teeth looked like they could sparkle.

"What... Are... You... Doing... Here?" I panted, trying to catch my breath.

"What do you mean? I always come to class."

"Right," I snorted. He nodded towards the classroom.

"Do you want to go in or...?"

"Wouldn't it be weird if went in at the same time? People might think that we came to school together."

Killian glanced at his watch.

"Oh look, it's 7:59."

My eyes widened and I opened the door.

"I'm sorry for being late!" I blurted. Everyone turned towards us, furrowing their eyebrows when they saw me and Killian standing at the entrance.

"We," Killian smiled casually. "He meant we."

"It's fine, Carter, I was just about to start roll call," Mr. Peten said, looking just as confused as everyone else. "Take a seat."

Everyone stared at us as we walked in, shocked by the unexpected duo. I sat down beside Eshe while Killian went to the very back.

"Why did you come with Killian?" Eshe whispered.

"It was a coincidence," I whispered. Eshe studied my face, pursed her lips, but didn't say anything. The bell rang and class ended. I knew something was wrong when Eshe left the classroom without me. I had to run to catch up to her.

"Eshe, wait up!"

She stopped and turned around, her arms crossed over her chest.

"What?" she snapped coldly.

"Are you upset?"

"What would I be upset about? The fact that you smoked, almost came late to class, or that you hung out with Killian last night without telling me?"

My eyes widened. "How did you—"

"Anna wouldn't stop talking about your smoking hot classmate. Since when were you friends with Killian?"

"Are you upset that Killian helped me look for your cat?" I asked. Eshe's jaw tightened then she sighed.

"No," she admitted. "I just feel like you've changed since you got detention."

★* Y.O.L.O - I.J Hidee ★*

"What do you mean?"

"We normally tell each other everything. Now I feel like you're hiding things from me. And I told you not to get too close to Killian." She narrowed her eyes at me. "Don't tell me you're starting to grow feelings for him."

"No!" But my face turned bright red. Eshe saw past my lie and tilted her head back with a groan. She planted her hands on my shoulders and gave me a gentle shake.

"Carter, I'm telling you this because I love you and I don't want you to get hurt. But you and Killian? That's never going to happen."

I flinched at her words.

"Killian doesn't care about you. In fact, he probably doesn't care about anyone but himself. Do you know how many girls got their hearts broken because of him?"

"He's not a bad person!" I quickly argued, but then I remembered the text he received from a girl named Amber yesterday.

"Do you hear yourself right now?" she asked. "I know I might seem like the bad guy and that you don't want to hear what I'm saying, but I'm trying to protect you. You're speaking through emotions. I'm stating facts. Have you ever seen him in a relationship?"

I was about to say something but remembered what he told me the first day we had detention together.

'I'm saying I'm a horny teenager who likes to sleep around. I'm a good friend, the ride or die type of guy. But as a boyfriend? I'm absolute shit. Heck, I wouldn't even date myself.'

" You might think you're special, but he treats you the way he treats everyone else. Just because he's nice, doesn't mean he's into you."

She spun me around and nodded towards Killian who was chatting with two pretty girls. They were giggling and twisting their ponytails, looking at him with dreamy looks in their eyes.

"See? That's who he really is," Eshe said, and I felt myself crumble inside.

***

I was in detention, staring at my notes. I couldn't stop thinking about what Eshe said to me this morning. Did I really have feelings for Killian?

'You and Killian? That's never going to happen.'

Eshe was right. Killian and I were too different.

The door squeaked open. Killian came in thirty minutes late as usual. He sat down beside me with the same cheerful smile on his face.

"Hey Jones," he chirped.

"Hi," I answered flatly.

Killian unwrapped a lollipop and popped it in his mouth.

"It's a good replacement for cigarettes," he told me.
"You're replacing lung cancer with diabetes?"

"Now there's the blunt Jones that I know and love," he chuckled. My chest tightened and my stomach fluttered. Love? No, no, don't get the wrong idea, Carter. It's just a figure of speech. But my heart wouldn't stop racing.

"Did something bad happen today? You look stressed." He looked at me. "More than usual."

"No, nothing bad happened," I mumbled.

"You sure?"

I didn't answer and stared at my notes.

"You don't have to tell me if you don't want to," he said.

It felt weird because my friends and family would normally pressure me into talking even if I didn't want to. But instead of bombarding me with questions, Killian took out his science book and started studying.

Ten minutes later, he stood up and started doing squats out of the blue. He sat back down, but his leg kept bouncing as he spun his pencil in his hand. Another few minutes later, he stood up again and started doing push-ups. He sat down, looked at his textbook, then groaned, pressing his forehead against the table.

"Are you okay?" I asked worriedly. He tilted his head towards me with a pout.

"I don't understand any of this."

"Which part?"

He lifted his head and pointed at the first page.

"This," he said. Oh, well if it's just that— "And this." He flipped to the next page. "And this, and this, and this..."

He flipped through the entire first chapter and I let out a nervous chuckle. Then again, when you only came to class once or twice a week, there were bound to be consequences.

"I'll help you," I suggested, scooting my chair closer to his. "You can start by learning the definition of the triple point. It's bound to appear on our quiz."

"What if I don't understand the definition?" He asked, already sounding irritated.

"Then I'll explain it to you," I said softly. "The triple point is when water boils and freezes at the same time. The temperature and pressure are just right for the three phases, which are?"

"Gas, liquid, and solid," he said. I nodded encouragingly. "So, the temperature and pressure are just right for those three phases of to coexist in a thermodynamic equilibrium."

"Thermo— What?"

"Thermodynamic equilibrium," I repeated slowly, helping him write it down. "It's when a system is in a thermal, mechanical and chemical equilibrium, all at the same time, which allows water to freeze and boil at the same time."
I continued to explain it until he finally understood.

"Wow, Jones, you're really good at this. If you were my teacher, I'd come to school every day," he said. I laughed nervously, shifting my gaze.

No, Carter! Remember what Eshe said. You shouldn't fall for Killian. You'll only get hurt.

"You seem to like it when I praise you," he mused with a playful look in his eyes that made me blush even more.

"N-No, I—" was a stuttering mess.

Killian leaned his jaw against his fist with a feline smile.

"There, there, no need to be shy. We all have our own little kinks," he winked, making me blush furiously. I looked away and pretended to write something down when really, I was just scribbling random words.

"Stop teasing me and study," I mumbled hoarsely.

Killian laughed.

"Yes, sir."

I could have sworn he saluted.

★* Y.O.L.O - I.J Hidee ★*

Chapter 14: Tutorial on How to Forget Your Crush

My mom knocked on the door and came into my room, looking over my shoulder to make sure that I was studying.

"Hey sweetie," she chirped, putting a plate of baby carrots on my desk. "Don't overwork yourself, okay?"

I forced a small smile.

"Yeah," I mumbled.

Mom told me that she and dad had to work, and that dinner was in the fridge. She kissed me on the head before leaving. As soon as she closed the door, my smile dropped and I slumped in my seat, resting my cheek on my notebook. A voice echoed inside my mind.

'Don't you ever tired of being good?'

"I do," I mumbled to myself. I looked at my hand and frowned as I curled and uncurled my fingers, feeling like something was missing. The memory of holding Killian's hand suddenly popped up in my mind. I remembered how big and warm they felt. I wanted to hold his hand again.

I took out my laptop and typed into the search bar: *Ways to get forget your crush.*

I clicked the first website which was *Wikihow*. It wasn't the most reliable source, but I was desperate.

> 1. *Let your emotions out. If you want to forget your crush, then the first thing you have to do is to admit that you have strong feelings for this person. If you're in denial about how much your crush means to you, then you'll just keep all of those intense feelings inside instead of letting them go.*

I picked up Kiwi and sat him on my desk, putting my hands against his fluffy cheeks. I took in a deep breath.

"I like Killian," I blurted aloud. I blinked a few times, feeling the heat slowly rise into my neck.

Okay, what was next?

> 2. *Forget your anger and bitterness. You may have many reasons for feeling angry or bitter.*

It was true that I'd been feeling rather bitter. I needed to get rid of the negative energy, but jealousy was something that I couldn't control, so I decided to skip the second step.

> 3. *Focus on your crush's worst qualities. Stop thinking about how good-looking, funny, or sweet your crush is whenever they pop in your mind. Instead, focus on all of the bad parts about your*

crush, from their weird fashion sense or their ability to be mean to perfect strangers.

I grabbed a blank piece of paper and pen and decided to make a list, writing down whatever came to mind. Killian's bad traits. Let's see...

-honest
-kind
-mysterious
-handsome
-has a good great smile
-pistachio-colored eyes
-smells nice

I read the bullet notes and then added:

-big, warm hands

I re-read my notes and frowned. No, this didn't look right. I scrunched up the piece or paper in frustration and threw it over my shoulder, grabbing a new sheet of paper and tried again.

-ditches class
-irresponsible
-swears (sometimes)
-flirts with everyone

But none of his flaws made me dislike him.

"None of this is working," I moaned miserably. So I decided to look up *'How to get your mind off of things'* and clicked on the first website.

Exercise. *Getting just 30 minutes a day of healthy exercise will help relax your body.*

I wasn't a big fan of exercising or doing anything that required physical effort, but after nibbling the back of my pen and debating on what I should do, I decided to go for a jog. I put on a baggy shirt, tucked it into my shorts, and slapped on a neon yellow headband. I put my hands on my hips and looked at myself in the mirror, nodding in self-satisfaction.

"I look good," I grunted in self-satisfaction. I stretched my hips and heard a bone crack. That didn't sound right.

After warming up, I grabbed my phone and headed out. The jog felt refreshing at first, but about five minutes later, I was panting and wheezing like a dying walrus. I collapsed on someone's front lawn and stared at the bright blue sky. It made me think of how Killian and I gazed at the sky as he walked me home.

I moaned, putting my hands over my eyes.

"This isn't supposed to happen."

I rolled to my side, hugging my knees against my chest, poking a strand of grass.

Maybe I should avoid him at school. Well, it wasn't like he came to school that often, so it shouldn't be that hard, right? All I had to do was avoid him in detention. Besides, we only had two dares left. After that, there was no reason for us to speak.

But the thought of not being able to be around him upset me. Would things change between us after our bet ended? Would Killian and I go back to being strangers? But what if I didn't want to be strangers.

I sat up, shaking my head.

I needed to get rid of my feelings before this got any worse. Eshe was right, falling for him was a mistake.

"Yeah, I'll just avoid him," I grunted with a determined nod.
My phone rang and my heart leaped inside my chest.
It was Killian. The universe was not making this easy for me, was it?

"Hello?" I answered.

"Hey, Jones. Why are you out of breath?" There was a pause. "Oh, my bad, am I interrupting you?"

My eyes widened and I felt my face turn bright red. Why did everyone assume that I was doing something sexual?!

"No!" I blurted. "I just finished a long jog."

A long jog was an overstatement. I could see my house from here. I cleared my voice and tried to speak in a serious tone.

"Killian, we need to talk," I declared.

"Yes?" he asked in a sugary sweet tone.

"I think we should stop calling each other. I'm not allowed to answer the phone unless it's important."

"But I am important, aren't I?"

I took in a sharp breath and looked down at my chest with narrowed eyes, poking it with my index.

No, heart, stop that!

"What do you want Killian?" I asked in a strained voice.

"I thought of your third dare. Have you ever been to a party?"

I was slightly offended. "Of course, I have."

"When I say party, I don't mean a birthday party that you threw back when you were in kindergarten," he clarified.

"Then of course I haven't. Do you know how dangerous teenage parties are?"

"Dangerous?"

"Yes" I said. "Isn't there always drugs and alcohol?"

"Not always, but most of the time, yeah."

"I have better things to do than intoxicate myself with people I hardly know."

"Better things? Like studying for a science test or reading a book by Charles Dickens?"

I gasped.

"How dare you? Charles Dickens is a great writer, thank you very much."

"You're very welcome," he beamed. "Come on, Jones, you're seventeen! Parties aren't as bad as you think. You'll can make new friends. Though, I can't guarantee that there will be good music."

I pressed my lips together.

"Will I have to drink alcohol?" I asked in a small voice.

"Only if you want to."

"Will there be juice?"

"I'll buy you juice."

I fiddled with my fingers, contemplating.

"And you'll be there?"

"Yes, I'm the one taking you," he laughed.

"Alright then, I'll go."

"Perfect," he beamed. "Oh, and make sure to wear something nice."

My jaw dropped open. "I always dress nice!"

"You dress like a grandpa."

"What's wrong with that? Grandpas are hip."

"The fact that you said hip makes it worse," he chuckled.

"If you think that I'm going to wear a Nike sweater, ripped skinny jeans and a pair of Timberlands, then the door is over there," I said. I pointed at the tree beside me which wasn't exactly a door, but doors were made of wood, so I assumed it was close enough.

"You can pick something out in my closet," he said.

"*Your* closet?" I asked, confused.

"I'll send you my address. I'll see ya later."

Before I could stop him, he hung up. A few seconds later, I received his address through text. I stared at my screen.

Maybe this was going to be harder than I thought.

Chapter 15: My Life

I stopped at the door, taking in a deep breath before knocking. My back straightened when someone opened it. A beautiful lady with light brown hair and bright green eyes stood in front of me. Her eyes looked just like Killian's, except they were a shade brighter.

"Hello, I'm looking for Killian Henderson. I'm his classmate, Carter," I said nervously. Maybe she was his older sister?

"Oh, it's nice to meet you, Carter. I'm Killian's mom," she smiled warmly. My lips parted. Nope, she was his mom.

She looked over her shoulder.

"Killian, your classmate is here to see you!" she called.

"I'll be down in a sec!" he answered from above.

"You can wait inside," she said, inviting me in. There were pictures of Killian and his mom on the beige walls. The walls were also decorated with paintings. Memorable portraits, breathtaking landscapes, some were just splashes of colors, but they were all beautiful.

"Killian painted those," Mrs. Henderson said, and I looked at her in surprise. "Killian loved art ever since he was a kid."

I didn't know that Killian liked art or that he painted. Now that I thought about it, I didn't know much about him.

"He doesn't look like a crafty, art kid, does he?" she chuckled, reading the expression on my face. I laughed nervously.

"No, not really," I admitted.

"Is he still going around acting like the cool kid at school?"

Um, he doesn't really come to school, I thought to myself.

"Don't be fooled by his appearance. He's not that cool if you ask me," she whispered. I giggled.

"You don't believe me?" She came back and brought a big binder. "Look at these."

I opened the first page and I smiled at Killian's baby pictures. There was one where he was sitting in a tub full of rubber duckies.

"This one's my favorite," she said, pulling at the one where Killian was sitting on a branch. The sky was a swirl of bright oranges and pink. He pointed at the sky with a wide, happy grin on his face. He looked like he was ready to conquer the world.

"He wouldn't come down no matter how many times I asked. He's always been like that," she sighed, but smiled. I could tell she loved him a lot. "You can keep it if you want. Oh, but don't tell Killian."

"Didn't you say this one was your favorite?" I frowned.

"You seem to like it more than I do," she winked.

We heard footsteps and I quickly slid the picture into my back pocket. Killian narrowed his eyes at the photo binder and tilted his head back with a groan.

"Mom, I told you not to show him my baby pictures."

"I couldn't help it," she said innocently. "You were so cute when you were little. I sometimes wonder where your chubby cheeks went."

"I hit puberty," he said. He looked at me and gave me a sly smile. "And I became hot, right Jones?"

My eyes widened and I quickly averted his gaze, too shy to answer in front of his mom.

"Oh please," Mrs. Henderson said, coming to my rescue. "Carter, honey, ignore him."

"Come on, Jones, we have to get ready," Killian said, taking my hand and pulling me up the stairs. I thanked his mom. I didn't know why, but I just felt like I had to.

"You seem close with your mom," I said.

"Yeah, she's the worst," he chuckled, showing me his room. I blinked in surprise. His floor was spotless, and his bed was made. I thought he'd have posters of models or soccer players hanging on the wall. Instead, there were beautiful paintings, most likely drawn by him.

"It's so tidy," I said.

"Why do you think I took so long?" he laughed. "But uh, I'd avoid looking under the bed if I were you. You want to sit?"

He nodded towards his bed, and I stiffened.

"I um, no, thank you."

He rolled his eyes.

"Relax, it's clean," he reassured me, sitting down first. "I don't bring people home. The walls are so thin, my mom would probably hear everything." He shivered at the thought. "Yikes."

I sat down on the other side of the bed from him, pressing my clammy hands together. For some reason, I couldn't look him in the eyes, so I stared at the ceiling like a fool.

"So, now what?" I asked nervously.

"We fuck."

I sprung up in surprise and he burst into laughter, catching my wrist and sitting me back down.

"Relax, Jones, I was kidding. I told you I'd help you get ready for the party, didn't I? We'll start with your hair."

He came back with hair gel.

"This stuff smells funny," I complained.

"This stuff is going to give you the messy *I just woke up* look that girls dig." After running his hands through my hair a few times and some last finishing touches, he pulled away and made a square shape with his hands, looking through it with one eye as if it was a camera.

"Perfect."

I looked into the mirror and was surprised by how nice my hair looked.

"You like it?" he grinned proudly. I nodded, blinking a few times to make sure that the person in the mirror was actually me.

"Hey, is your eyesight bad? I think it's the first time I've seen you without glasses," he said, studying my face. I awkwardly rubbed the nape of my neck, shifting my gaze.

"No, not really. I only wear them at school or when I study."

"Is your eyesight bad because you're always studying?"

I gave him a small nod, fiddling with my sleeves. He leaned against the wall. He peered past me, looking at one of his paintings, and for a moment, said nothing. Then, he said: "I know it's not my place to say this, but maybe studying so much isn't healthy for you."

My answer surprised me. "I do it for my parents."

I stared at the floor, pursed my lips, then met his gaze. He was looking at me now. Killian stared at me like I was a painting, looking deep into my eyes as if to search for a soul. His green eyes held a glimmer of compassion. They softened in the light, and at that moment, I felt like I could tell him everything.

"You're lucky you're close with your mom. I wish I had that with mine. My parents and I never talk about anything besides school and work."

Something in his eyes changed.

"She had me when she was a teen."

My eyes widened.

"Her ex left when she refused to get an abortion. Honestly, there's no stopping her once she sets her mind something," he chuckled darkly. "So yeah, we're close."

I pursed my lips.

"Don't look at me like that. I don't really care if I don't have a dad, it's not like I knew him or anything. You can't miss someone you don't know." Even though Killian said he didn't care, the tone of his voice altered. He looked away, staring out the window.

"It was for the best if you ask me. Having a dad like him would have sucked anyways."

When he looked at me, his eyes widened.

"Are you crying?"

"No," I quickly said, rubbing away my tears. Killian raised my chin and wiped them for me.

"Ah, jeez," he sighed. "If I knew I'd make you cry, I wouldn't have said any of that."

"I admire you and your mom. I can tell you two love each other a lot."

He blinked, then smiled.

"She's pretty great, isn't she?" he murmured. "Now stop crying, you're going to ruin your nice face."

I laughed nervously, wiping my lids. Even at moments like these, he was still flirty.

"You know why me and my mom are so close? It's because we argue and disagree. We say what's on our mind and we're honest with each other."

My brows furrowed.

"If you keep everything to yourself, your parents are never going to know how sad you are. They're going to keep bossing you around and make all your decisions for you. They think they're perfect while you're trying to be perfect. But if you ask me, a true relationship is when imperfect people refuse to give up on each other. Take my mom and I as exhibit A. And you know what, Jones? It's your life. It's okay to not want the same thing as your parents, so don't ever be sorry for that."

His words hit harder than I expected. Killian was right. This was *my* life. And maybe it was time I lived it that way.

Chapter 16: I Could Snap You in Half

Killian opened his closet. I reached for a sweater and put it against my chest to see if it would fit, but the sweater went well past my hips and the sleeves looked like they could eat up my entire hand.

"They're too big," I frowned. I studied Killian's body. He was taller and stronger, so of course his clothes wouldn't fit. He rubbed his jaw pensively.

"How tall are you?" he asked.

"How tall are *you*?" I asked, wanting to know his height first.

He grinned proudly. "I'm 6'2."

"I'm 5'6-ish," I said. He raised a brow, and I shifted my gaze. "Okay, I'm 5'5, but with shoes on, I can be 5'6."

"Cute," he smiled. "Here, try this."

He handed me a starch-white shirt with a baby chick printed on the front left pocket. I stared at him quizzically.

"I wore it when I was in 9th grade. It doesn't fit me anymore, but it was my favorite shirt."

"I thought you wanted to make me look cool."

"Hey, it is cool," he said defensively. "Girls loved it when I wore this shirt to school."

Yeah, they liked it because you wore it.

"What are you going to wear?" I asked.

"Any shirt will do," he shrugged. Without warning, he pulled his shirt over his head, revealing his bare torso. I gawked at his nice body, stunned. He wasn't the bulky type of muscular, but the lean and fit kind. He was perfect. I covered my eyes. I could hear him laugh.

"No need to be shy."

"I'm not," I mumbled. "But was it really necessary to take your shirt off so suddenly?"

"No, I just wanted to see your reaction," he chimed.

"Har, har, very funny. Are you done changing?"

"Yeah, you can look now."

But when I removed my hands, he was still shirtless. My eyes widened and I slapped his strong arm.

"I thought you said you were done changing!"

"What, you don't like my body?" he pouted, flexing his pecks, making me even more flustered. "C'mon Jones, I know you want to touch 'em."

"I don't. Now please cover up your man boobs. My eyes only accept pg-13 content."

"You don't even want to poke them?" he asked teasingly.

I gave it a quick poke, but my eyes widened at how hard they felt. I put both hands on his chest and looked up at him, amazed.

"They're so hard!" I gasped, squeezing his chest to make sure they were real. He smiled, but his cheeks turned slightly pink.

"Jones, your hands are on my nips," he grumbled huskily, and I immediately pulled away.

"Sorry," I stuttered, taking a step back. "I got carried away."

He put on a grey sweater, and I felt slightly disappointed.

"Aren't you going to change?" he asked.

"Can you turn around?" I asked, embarrassed to take my clothes off.

He raised a brow. "Really?"

"I'm shy," I murmured. He sighed but did as I asked. I attempted to take my shirt off just like Killian did, but my arms ended up getting tangled and I couldn't pull my shirt over my head. I struggled, then gave up. My arms felt numb.

"Killian?" I squeaked.

"Yeah?"

"I'm stuck."

A pause. "How?"

"I dunno."

"Do you want me to turn around and help?" he asked.

"Yes, please," I murmured. Killian helped me untangle my arms, and I winced when he tried to pull the sweater over my head.

"Does it hurt?" He asked worriedly.

"A bit," I admitted sheepishly. "Can you be gentler?"

"Right, sorry," he grunted, his voice strangely low and husky. He was more careful this time and successfully pulled the shirt over my head. I could finally see in front of me and could feel blood circulate back into the upper half of my body.

"Thanks," I smiled, but Killian was staring at my torso.

"Do you like my six-pack?" I said jokingly, rubbing the flat of my tummy. I always wanted a six-pack, but no matter how many crunches I did (which, I had to admit, weren't that many), my stomach remained as flat as a board.

"Um, Killian?" I asked, wondering why he was looking at me like that. It was the same look wolves had when they saw their prey.

My smile vanished when the atmosphere shifted. I sucked in a tight breath when he took a step closer towards me. He stood so close I could feel the warmth of his body. He reached out to touch me but stopped, and those magnetic pistachio-colored eyes focused on my face. When our gazes locked, I held my breath.

His head dipped slightly, and for one nerve-wracking second, I thought he was going to kiss me. I didn't pull away. To my dismay, his lips never reached mine.

"Can I touch you?" he asked. There was a chord of intensity in his voice that made me gulp.

I mean, I had touched him, so it was only fair if I let him touch me.

"Yeah," I squeaked. He put his big hands on my waist and pulled me closer. I staggered forward and pressed my hands against his chest. He felt hard.

"You're so slim," he murmured in a daze, making me blush even more. The baritone of his voice echoed through my ears and sent a tingly feeling down my spine. I let out a sheepish laugh, trying to remain calm when I was seconds away from having a panic attack.

His hands slowly slid up my small waist and I bit my lower lip to hold back a whimper.

"Killian," I begged in a strained voice, biting down on my lower lip as his hands continued to travel up my body. "What are you doing?"

But Killian seemed too distracted.

"So frail," he said, his minty breath dancing against my skin. The tingling sensation started to grow, and my toes curled on the rug. I didn't know what was happening to me. I felt hot and achy, and I wanted to touch me more.

He stopped at my chest and gave it a small squeeze. I muffled a moan. He lowered his lips to my ear and whispered, "I could just snap you in half."

★* Y.O.L.O - I.J Hidee ★*

Chapter 17: Do You Like Me?

Snap me in- What?!

A flurry of shivers skittered through me, and the heat of his body seared into me. His divine scent wasn't helping at all. Before I could give into my out-of-control hormones, I pulled myself out of his grip with unnecessary force and staggered back. The sudden movement snapped Killian back to his senses because he retrieved his hand.

"Jones—"

"I'll be downstairs," I blurted, dashing for the door. He caught my wrist, and I pulled away with an alarmed look in my eyes. He released me and raised his hands to prove that he wouldn't touch me again. He licked his lips, shifted his gaze, then ran a hand through his as if he didn't know what else to do with them.

"You should put on a shirt," he said quietly.

Which was when I realized that I was still shirtless. I covered my nips even though Killian had already seen them. He turned around without me having to ask this time and I quickly put on my clothes.

I went downstairs first and pressed my back against the wall, feeling my heart hammering against my chest.

Calm down, Carter, a voice in my head said. *He was just admiring your body, that was all he was doing.*

I closed my eyes.

Don't look into it too much. You guys are just classmates, so just act cool.

When I heard Killian's footsteps, I spun around and faced the wall.

"Jones, just because you can't see me, doesn't mean I can't see you," I heard him say.

"I'm admiring your wall. You have a nice wall. What color is this?"

He was quiet for a moment, then said, "White."

I squeezed my eyes shut.

"Is this because of what happened upstairs?" he asked, coming closer.

"The party!" I exclaimed. "We're going to be late."

I turned around and was surprised to see Killian standing right behind me. The image of his strong, broad chest flashed through my mind, and my cheeks turned red. He opened his mouth to say something, but I brushed past him and left the house. I knew I was acting weird, but how could

I not? Killian just told me how small and frail I was and how he could just snap me in half!

Killian unlocked his jeep and I climbed into the passenger's seat. I tried to put my seatbelt on, but it was stuck.

"You have to tug harder," Killian instructed. I tried again, but it wouldn't budge.

"Killian," I frowned before I could stop myself. I grew the habit of always asking him for help.

"Yeah, I got you." He leaned towards me. His body was so close to mine and his scent invaded my nostrils. I pressed my back against the seat so our faces wouldn't touch. Hopefully, he wouldn't notice my double chin.

He tugged and strapped the seatbelt around me.

"Is it too loose?"

I shook my head.

"Good," he grunted. "I like it better when they're tight."

"What?" I asked, confused.

"Oh, nothing, I was just talking to myself," he said dismissively, driving down the road. He broke the silence first.

"Do you have any girl friends apart from Eshe?"

"No, why?"

He didn't answer, and my chest was filled with excitement. Could it be that he was jealous?

"If you want, I can introduce you to some girls tonight."

And then my chest deflated.

"I know a girl who's a big fan of Charles Dickens," he carried on, worsening the pain in my chest. "I'm sure you two will get along."

My gaze dropped to my lap and my stomach went rigid. It felt like he was insinuating something.

"Yeah, maybe." I bit my lower lip. "Killian?"

"Mhm?"

"You said you don't do stable relationships, right?"

His jaw tightened. "Yeah, why?"

"Do you think that'll ever change?" I asked, trying not to sound hopeful. He was quiet for a moment, I thought he wasn't going to answer.

"No, not any time soon." A terrible knot twisted my heart. We stopped at a red light and his gaze locked with mine. He almost looked apologetic, which only made me feel worse.

"I'm not good at commitment unless it's with friends or family."

"Why?"

His voice was suddenly cold. "It's just how I am."

"Then for your third dare," I said. "You can't date someone unless you're planning on staying with them, at least, not until our bet is over."

He cocked a brow.

"That's a high request, Jones. May I ask your source of inspiration?"

My answer was plain and simple.

"No."

He chuckled darkly, running a hand through his hair. I didn't think he'd agree.

"Alright, I accept the dare," he finally said, and hope bloomed in my chest. "But can I ask you something?"

I always got nervous whenever someone asked if they could ask me something before actually asking the question. It normally meant they were going to ask something that they normally wouldn't

"Sure," I said. We stopped at another red light. His eyes flickered towards me.

"Do you like me?"

My spine straightened. A million questions invaded my head.

What do I do? Do I tell him the truth?

But the risk of losing him was too big, and I didn't want to lose the only person who understood me, or at least tried to.

"I appreciate your presence," I answered, unable to meet his gaze. "The light is green."

Killian stepped on the pedal. The silence that hung between us was killing me.

"I'm glad," he said, his voice as clear as day. I felt that same twinge of pain in my chest. "Falling for someone like me won't do you any good, but I don't need to worry about you. You're Carter Jones, and Carter Jones never goes around looking for trouble, right?"

I forced a smile but felt myself crumbling inside. I stared out the window.

"Right," I whispered.

Who knew liking someone would be so painful?

★* Y.O.L.O - I.J Hidee ★*

Chapter 18: Keep Your Hoe Hands Off of Him

We arrived at the party. When we drove into the neighborhood, you could immediately tell which house it was. You could hear music blasting from the inside. There was a bunch of teenagers in front of the house, jumping up and down like huddled-up Tic-Tacs shaking inside a box.

"Relax, Jones, you look constipated," he said easily, gently nudging my arm. We got out of his jeep, and I could already smell the alcohol and cigarettes. Strangers who looked too old to be teenagers wobbled past us, puking in the bushes behind. I inched closer towards Killian, my arm brushing against his biceps.

"I want to go home," I said stiffly.

"Relax, this stuff happens all the time," he reassured me.

When I didn't answer, he glanced at me. "You look pale."

"I feel pale."

"I didn't know pale was a feeling," he chuckled. I gave him a weak smile.

"Me neither."

"Don't worry. I'm here with you, aren't I?" he said, loosening the knots in my shoulders. "Nothing bad will happen."

"That's exactly what people say *before* something bad happens."

"Do you really want to go home?" he asked, his tone light but serious.

"I don't want to lose the bet."

Before he could answer, someone screamed his name.

"KILLIAAAAAAAN!" My eyes widened when a girl pounced on top of him, smacking his cheek with a kiss. I blinked in surprise, unsure about how I felt.

"I didn't think you were coming," she said, rubbing her cheek against Killian's face. Her brown hair was tied into a ponytail, and she had freckles on her button nose. Her long lashes were coated with mascara, framing her blue eyes. Yup, she was beautiful. I was now convinced that all of Killian's friends were secretly models.

"Jenna, get off of me. You're heavy," Killian grumbled. Jenna gasped, putting her hands on her hips.

"You do not tell a dainty, fancy lady that she is heavy!"

Killian looked around him.

"Lady? Where?" His eyes then stopped on Jenna. "All I see is a gorilla."

My lips parted and they started to fight and bicker, but you could tell it was a friendly fight. Well, I hoped it was. Killian headlocked Jenna who shrieked as she struggled in his grasp. She then bit his arm and Killian hissed in pain.

"Guys, please don't fight," I said, trying to break them apart. Jenna was still biting Killian's flesh when she looked up at me, her lashes fluttering in surprise. She released Killian's arm and slipped out of his grasp.

"Who are you?" she asked.

"This is Jo— Uh, I mean Carter." He gave me a sheepish smile. "Habits."

He then nodded towards Jenna.

"Carter, this is Gorilla. Er, I mean, Jenna."

Jenna stabbed him with a dark glare, but Killian raised a shoulder.

"Habits," he simply said.

She gave Killian a look of disgust but when she turned towards me, her expression lit up.

"Hi, Carter, I'm Jenna," she beamed, turning into a completely different person. Before she could shake my hand, Killian slapped it away.

"Keep your hoe hands off of him. This boy is precious," he said, and my heart did a funny little dance. Jenna rolled her eyes.

"That's rich coming from someone who switches partners quicker than his socks," she smirked.

We heard a chant of *'oooooh's'* coming from behind. A group of boys came over and greeted Killian with rough pushes and slaps. I wasn't sure if they were greeting him or trying to break his arm.

Luke was amongst the jocks, and I immediately felt out of place. These were the popular guys at our school, which reminded me that I didn't belong in the same circle.

"You actually came," Luke said. He was shorter than Killian but tall enough to be the captain of our school's football team. In fact, they were *all* tall. I felt like I was standing amongst a forest of trees with hair instead of leaves.

I hid behind Killian, but Luke's hawk eyes narrowed at me.

"And you brought a nerd?" he mocked. I flinched and his friends laughed. Being made fun of in front of your crush had to be the worst thing ever.

"It was better than coming with you," Killian said smoothly. The guys let out a louder, 'oooooh,' jumping up and down all hyped.

"Piss off."

"Where's Francis?" Killian asked.

"How the fuck should I know?"

"Well—"

Luke didn't let him finish.

"Whatever, will you just come with me? My cousin has been begging me to bring you to her."

Killian blinked blankly. "You have a cousin?"

Luke punched him in the arm.

"Yeah, you fucked her last month, doofus," Luke snapped. My eyes widened, but Killian's eyes remained indifferent.

"If it was last month, then why does she want to see me now?"

"You owe her that much after treating her like trash. If you weren't my friend, I would've already beaten you to a pulp."

"Wow, hang on there," Killian said, raising a hand. "First of all, I didn't treat her like trash. I specifically told her that it was a one-night stand and she agreed. It's not my fault if she expected more. Secondly, only in your dreams would you be able to beat me in a fight. And thirdly," said Killian, cocking a brow. "We're friends?"

The boys went wild.

"Will you just come with me?" Luke sighed. "I don't have time for this. Francis is waiting for me, and I can't be with him if my cousin is calling me every five minutes whining about how my best friend fucked her over."

"I'm watching over Jones," Killian said.

"The nerd?" Luke sneered. "Since when did you babysit?"

I flinched.

"It's fine," I quickly said. I didn't want Killian to leave, but I also didn't want him to stay. Killian turned towards me with a stern look in his eyes. "You should go."

"No, I'm not leaving you," he said firmly.

"I'll be okay."

"I promised to look after you."

"I'm not a kid," I snapped. The tone of my voice surprised both of us.

"Are you sure?" His tone was casual. Unaffected. But the atmosphere between us shifted.

"Yeah."

He pursed his lips, hesitated, then turned towards Jenna.

"Hey, J, I'll be back in a few minutes so take care of him until then, okay?"

"I thought you said to keep my hoe hands away from him," she snorted.

"I said to take care of him, not touch him," he growled as he was being dragged away by Luke and his friends. "Jones is a precious boy who must remain innocent and untainted," he yelled as he started to get further and further away. "Don't give him any alcohol or drugs, and I swear, if anyone-"

His voice was muffled by the music, and he disappeared into the crowd of half-drunk teens who were dancing. Or at least, trying to.

"Since when did he start acting so responsible?"

"Are Killian and Luke really friends?" I asked worriedly.

She chuckled. "Yeah, but the girls go crazy over them. They even have their own ship name," she cackled. "Some people called them Lilian, others call them Kuke."

"Kuke?" I asked confusingly. *It sounded like puke.*

"I know," she laughed. "Anyway, you must be thirsty. How about we head inside and grab a drink?"

"Do you guys have juice?" I asked nervously, following her into the house. The smile on her face made me slightly anxious.

"Sure," she grinned.

★* Y.O.L.O - I.J Hidee ★*

Chapter 19: Never Have Expectations

Jenna started mixing different drinks into a bright red cup and stirred it with a fork before handing it to me. I looked down at the murky color. My nose wrinkled at the fruity, acidic, bitter odor.

"I don't drink," I said as politely as I could. She rolled her blue eyes.

"Everybody drinks."

The last time I drank was Christmas with my parents, and that was only a sip of champagne.

"Alcohol isn't good for the brain," I said, but Jenna already took a shot of vodka.

"And global warming is killing the planet," she said, wiping her lips with the back of her hand as she poured herself another drink. "Carter, humans are born to be self-destructive. We're the only living species with suicidal tendencies. Live up to your uniqueness and drink up."

"But Killian told me not to drink."

"And you're going to listen to the guy who listens to no one else but himself?" She snorted.

I hesitated at first. I guess one sip wouldn't hurt. My face scrunched at how bitter and awful it tasted, but Jenna was standing in front of the sink so I couldn't spit it out. The liquid sizzled down my throat and burned my chest.

"Tastes like life, doesn't it?" she grinned widely. "So tell me, how long have you been sleeping with Killian?"

I gagged, and it wasn't because of the alcohol.

"We're not sleeping together."

She raised a brow. "Then what do you two do?"

"We hang out sometimes," I said. Jenna belted into laughter, shaking her head.

"No, you don't get it. Killian doesn't just *hang out* with people, not unless you're a ride-or-die friend like Francisco or Luke. You're either a fuck buddy or a waste of time."

For some reason, her words stung. I knew she wasn't trying to come off mean, but her words still hurt. I wanted to tell her that Killian and I were friends, but were we really? The only thing that kept us tied together was our bet.

"We're helping each other," I elaborated. "He's trying to be a better person and I'm trying to find out who I really am."

Jenna blinked blankly before bursting into another split of laughter.

"A better person? Who, Killian? Oh, please."

"How did you two meet?" I asked, eager to change the subject. H

"We met the way he meets most girls. At some dumb party I can hardly remember," she said, her voice suddenly bitter. "I was head-over-heels for him, so when he offered to sleep with me, I took the chance and said yes. I mean, who wouldn't? The rumors of him being a beast under the sheets had me hooked."

Beast under the sheets? Like a monster?

I tried to imagine Killian jumping out of the sheets and saying rawr.

Jenna must have read the confused expression on my face.

"I meant that he's good in bed," she clarified. And just in case I still didn't understand, she added, "He's kinky, but not in a creepy way, which is kind of hard to find because the number of dudes with feet fetishes? Hunny, no," she shuddered. "Killian is the right amount of kinky. He knows how to make you feel good and hits the right spot. Oh, and don't get me started with how big—"

"Did you two date?" I asked briskly. The expression on her face hardened and she took another shot of vodka.

"Like I said," she said, her voice hoarse. "Killian doesn't date. He fucks."
"Oh."

Jenna leaned against the counter, swirling her drink.

"I thought I was different. Girls have this dumb tendency to think that they can fix a boy and make them better. I thought I was special different from everyone else and that I actually had my chances, but he got bored of me after a few days and left me heartbroken. I can't even get mad at him because before I slept with me, he told me that he wanted nothing more than just a good time."

For a second, I see pain in her eyes.

"If you knew you'd get hurt, why did you agree?"

"You seem to make me repeat myself. Humans are the only living species that are self-destructive. Hell, I bet we're all just a bunch of masochists!" she said, throwing her hands in the air and spilling half her drink on the floor.

I could tell that she was getting tipsy. I tried to take the cup from her hand, but she finished it in one go.

"I thought I could change him, I really did. The way he treats you makes you feel special like you're the only one in the world. No one's ever made me feel like that." Her voice fell to a whisper and her eyes unfocused. She looked away, but her voice was unsteady. "We're on good terms now. We're friends, sort of," she mumbled. "But that's all we are. That's all we're ever going to be."

I couldn't help but feel bad for her. But who was I to pity her? I was in the same position as she was. Jenna poured herself another drink. I tried to stop her, but she pushed me away and pointed a sharp finger at me. Her nails could be claws.

"Never stop a heartbroken girl from drinking," she warned me and drank straight out of the bottle. "Ugh, I hate him."

I knew she didn't mean it.

"He's that unattainable person that you can't help but fall for. No matter how badly you want him, you just can't. He's like a drug. You know he's bad for you, but you can't get enough of him."

"He's like a hot potato!" I blurted. She stared at me.

"Am I drunk, or did you just say that Killian was a hot potato?"

I chuckled nervously, rubbing the nape of my neck.

"When a hot potato comes out of the oven, you know how hot it is, but you still bite into it."

Jenna's face scrunched then the wrinkles on her face softened.

"That is one weird way to put it, but I guess I see what you mean."

She handed me the bottle of vodka and I drank from the bottle. I took a gulp and pulled away with a scowl, but it didn't taste as bad it first did.

"Um, Jenna?" I croaked, my voice raspy.

"Yeah?"

"If you could go back in time, what would you tell yourself?" I asked, hoping I wasn't being too transparent. Her face hardened and the empty tone of her voice left me stunned.

"Never have expectations."

I stared at her wondering if she was the same girl who tackled Killian with a wide grin. She clapped her hands together and she put on a smile.

"Enough of this depressing chit-chat. We're here to partaaay!" she hooted, swaying her lips side-to-side. "Let's go play a round of beer pong!"

She grabbed my hand and pulled me out of the kitchen, threading me through the crowd of people.

"But Killian—"

Jenna looked over her shoulder.

"Screw that jerk. You and I are going to have some fun!"

★* Y.O.L.O - I.J Hidee ★*

Chapter 20: Got the Moves Like Jagger

"Drink, drink, drink, drink!" the crowd chanted. I picked up my fifth cup of beer and chugged it, scrunching my face at the bitter taste before flipping the cup over my head. Only a few drops came out, and the crowd went wild.

"Whoohoo!" I hooted, giggling like there was no tomorrow. I couldn't believe I was ever nervous about coming to the party tonight because holy macaroni, I was having a blast!

Jenna put a ping pong ball in my hand. My vision was blurry, and I could hardly stand straight, let alone, focus on my aim. But I tossed the ball anyway and it went in.

Another thunder of applaud and hoots broke out. Jenna jumped up and down in excitement, pulling me into her arms and squeezing the life out of me. I almost puked on her shoulder, but I managed to swallow it down.

I knew I was drunk when the alcohol stopped tasting so bad. My brain was sending me warning signals, telling me to sit down and rest, but my limbs had a mind of their own. Everything felt slowed down. I was moving, but in delay, and I couldn't focus on a single thing. There were three

★* Y.O.L.O - I.J Hidee ★*

Jenna's standing in front of me and I burst into a hysterical fit of giggles. I walked over towards her but tripped over nothing, catching myself before landing flat on my face. I was drunk. No, I was free.

We lost the second round of beer pong and Jenna and I had to drink the remaining cups of beer for both teams as a penalty. I felt nauseous and sick, but that didn't stop me from going to the living room with the rest of the drunk kids.

I wanted to dance. I wanted to party. I wanted to *live*.

Jenna danced beside me. Me? I was violently flailing my arms an inflatable tube man at a gas station. People were filming me on their phones, but I didn't care. I normally would, but I didn't right now. It felt good not caring. I didn't give a single dingle.

I climbed onto the table and began busting out some moves.

"Go, Carter, go Carter, go, go, go Carter!" the crowd cheered.

I did the running man, and the crowd went wild.
When I started doing the sprinkler, everyone in the living room mimicked me and was busting out moves from the 90's. Jenna was laughing so hard she fell to the floor, pounding her fists against the rug.

After some hardcore dancing, I started to lose my breath and decided to rest on the couch. I must have jumped around too much because I felt nauseous, and my head hurt. Everything around me spun like a merry-go-round and I knew it was time to stop. I clutched my waist and let out a miserable groan, tilting my head back in hopes that I wouldn't puke.

Jenna plopped down beside me, and the sudden movement made me groan.

"What time is it?" I croaked.

"It's still early," she reassured me. I felt relieved.

"Oh."

"It's 11:50 p.m."

My eyes shot open, and I suddenly felt sober. "What?!"

Jenna cupped her hands around her mouth.

"I said it's 11:50 p.m," she yelled into my face.

It was way past my curfew, and my parents were going to be home in ten minutes. I needed to find Killian and get home before they did.

"I have to go," I blurted, quickly standing up, but sitting back down.

"Are you okay?" Jenna asked.

I closed my eyes and felt my eyes swivel to the back of my head. I blinked hard, but nothing would remain still.

"I feel terrible," I admitted, feeling tears prick my eyes. I regretted drinking so much and just wanted to be okay again.

"Here, this will make you feel better," she said, slipping something into my mouth. I swallowed without a second thought.

"What was it?"

"It'll make you feel good," she reassured me. I was too drunk to worry about the pill. Besides, Killian trusted Jenna, so so should I. Speaking of which, where was he? I haven't seen him since he left with Luke.

"I need to find him," I said with a sudden burst of determination.

You want to find him, my consciousness corrected.

"Oh, hush," I spoke to myself, bonking the side of my head. I probably looked crazy. I stood up. Well, I thought I stood up, but I realized that my head was resting on Jenna's shoulder. I felt worse each second.

"Jenna, I want to go home," I moaned.

"Shhh," she hushed. "Close your eyes and just relax."

She caressed my hair, her gentle touch making me shiver. I felt like I was being hypnotized. There was a strange tingling sensation that spread through my body. It felt different from when I drank alcohol. Not only that, but I could also feel my blood circulate quickly down my waist, making me shift side-to-side as my lower member slowly started to swell.

"Do you feel it?" she asked.

I didn't know what she meant by *it*, but I could feel my boxer's getting uncomfortably tight. She looked down and I quickly tried to pull down my shirt to hide it, my cheeks flushing bright red. What was going on? Why was my body reacting this way and why couldn't I control myself?

"Don't worry, it's normal," she said smoothly, putting her hand on my leg. I bit my lower lip, everything below my waist starting to throb. This had to be the worst time to be getting an erection.

I wanted to stand up and leave, but my body wouldn't listen. To make things worse, I kept having dirty thoughts about Killian when it clearly wasn't the time to be fantasizing about him!

"Jenna, please stop," I begged as she continued to touch me in ways that made me uncomfortable. I felt frustrated and helpless, but Jenna was too drunk to listen.

"Come on, just enjoy it," she purred, giving my thigh a tight squeeze. A gasp escaped my throat. She pulled me onto her lap, leaning in to kiss me.

I was drunk, but not drunk enough to let my first kiss be stolen by a girl. I pulled my head back and slapped my hands on my lips.

"Oh, come on, don't be like that," she giggled, thinking that I was joking. We wrestled, and I was losing. She wrapped her arms around the back on my neck and was about to kiss me. I squeezed my eyes shut, accepting my fate.

Someone pulled me off the couch, jerking me to safety. My back hit the hardness of a familiar body, and I opened my eyes. Killian's hand tightened around mine, and he stood protectively in front of me.

And boy, did he look angry.

★* Y.O.L.O - I.J Hidee ★*

Chapter 21: Drunk Confession

"What the hell are you doing?" Killian's hissed through gritted teeth. I flinched at his harsh tone.

"We were just having fun," Jenna replied innocently. She put on a brave face, but I could tell she was intimidated by Killian too.

"I told you not to give him any alcohol," Killian spat.

"He only had a couple of sips."

"He's completely wasted!" Killian roared, his voice making my back straighten. His husky voice boiled with anger, and his grip tightened around my wrist. The pressure aroused me, and my erection worsened.

I tried to push away the dirty thoughts but failed terribly. Killian turned towards me. His green eyes clouded with worry as he studied my face. I looked away in embarrassment, lowering my shirt in hopes that he didn't notice.

"Killian, you're hurting me," I said in a small voice. His grip loosened, but only slightly. He turned back towards Jenna.

"What did you give him?" he asked, his voice as cold as a winter night.

Jenna shifted her gaze to the side. "Nothing, I—"

"Jenna," he sharply cut her off. "Cut the bullshit."

Jenna bit her lower lip, then sighed.

"Alright, I may or may not have given him a pill," she said. "And that pill may or may not have been Viagra."

My lips parted in shock and my stomach curled. The pill I took wasn't medicine, but Viagra?! No wonder my body was reacting this way!

Stunned, I stared at Jenna in confusion and betrayal. I trusted her. I thought she was my friend.

"It's not going to do him any harm!" Jenna said when nobody spoke. Her words felt like a physical punch in the stomach.

"You gave him alcohol *and* drugs? Does he even know what he took?" Killian demanded.

"Well, now he does," she mumbled. "What are you getting so worked up about anyway? It's not like you've never done it before!"

"Yeah, but unlike you, I actually do it with fucking consent," he snarled.

They continued to argue and fight, but the more time passed, the harder I got. My briefs tightened around my waist, and it hurt to stand. Killian's tight grip and husky voice weren't helping at all. I battled a rush of unease, swallowing the lump in my throat.

"Killian," I whined. "I'm hot."

I felt him stiffen. He wouldn't look me in the eyes. He ran his tattooed hand through his hair, muttered something under his breath, then his voice softened just slightly.

"Hang in there. We'll take care of it soon," he promised, giving me a gentle squeeze. I could tell he was trying to speak as calmly as he could. There was nothing sexier than a man who tried.

"Aren't you the one who's always going around saying Y.O.L.O?" Jenna demanded, grabbing his attention. "Why are you making me look like the bad guy here? I gave him Viagra, so what? We only live once anyway. At least he can die knowing he tried drugs once in his life."

"Are you being serious right now?" Killian scoffed, but Jenna was on a roll.

"And maybe he wouldn't be in this situation if you had just watched over him yourself." She cocked an eyebrow, a smug sneer twisting her lips. "Oh, but you were too busy getting into another girl's pants, weren't you?"

I flinched, turning towards Killian with a terrible ache in my chest. It wasn't like I haven't thought about that before. I mean, why else would he have taken so long? But I refused to believe it and hoped he didn't forget me.

But let's face it. I was a nerd with average looks and a low social ranking. Why did I keep thinking that I might have a chance with someone like Killian? He was way out of my league.

"Jenna, I'm not in the mood to be dealing with your jealousy right now, but if blaming me for your fucked up personality makes you feel good about yourself, then be my guest," he muttered coldly. "And you wonder why I ditched you after three days."

Shock registered on Jenna's face and pain flickered in her eyes. She sat there, speechless. Her eyes watered and her lower lip quivered. She stood up to leave, but Killian caught her arm and sat her back down.

"Let go!" Jenna screamed at him, but Killian had already released her. He pulled out his phone and called someone.

"Luke?" he said. "Jenna is drunk on the living room couch. I need you to drive her home."

My eyes widened in surprise. Even after Jenna's betrayal, Killian couldn't leave her in the vulnerable state she was in. She was drunk in a house full of more drunk teenagers, so of course he'd worry. I could hear Luke's muffled voice. He didn't seem very happy, not that he ever was.

"If she pukes in your car, I'll clean it up," Killian growled impatiently. "No, I can't do it myself. I have something more important to do."

His eyes flickered towards me and I blushed furiously. I stared at my feet.

"Yeah, I owe you one," Killian said. I think I heard Luke say 'shut up' before hanging up. Killian turned towards Jenna.

"Luke is going to take you home. He didn't drink or smoke, so you don't have to worry. Don't move from this couch until he gets here and don't trust anyone else but him. I swear if I hear that you went home with some wasted piece of trash..." His voice was quiet but cold. I thought it was cute how Killian was protective over her and understood why Jenna had feelings for him. I mean, how could she not?

"I don't need your help," she muttered.

"Yeah, you're welcome," Killian snorted.

Jenna swallowed hard and looked like she was trying her best not to burst into tears. She finally looked up at him, guilt swarming her bloodshot eyes.

"I'm sorry," she whispered.

"I'm not the one you should be apologizing too."

Killian took my hand and pulled me through the crowd. He was walking so quickly, I could hardly keep up.

"Killian, slow down," I begged, wincing as my hand was crushed inside his grip. "Slow down, you're going too fast!"

We went upstairs and he opened a random door. There were two girls and one guy on a bed, all of them butt naked. They shrieked in surprise and Killian covered my eyes.

"Jesus, people, get a room," Killian groaned, slamming the door shut.

We went into another room. This time, it was empty. He put his hands on my shoulders and sat me on the bed, raising my chin and studying my face. I pulled down the hem of my shirt. He must have noticed what I was doing.

"It's okay, Jones, you don't need to get embarrassed. It's the side effects," he said gently. "How do you feel?"

"My head feels like it's going to explode, and my body feels hot," I mumbled, pushing his hand away. Anything and anyone that touched me right now felt sexual. Killian put his hand on my forehead.

"You're burning up," he frowned. "How much did you drink?"

My eyes fell to my knees.

"Right," he mumbled. "Look, I'll leave the room so that you can take care of yourself. I'll take you home as soon as you're done."

He turned around to leave, but I caught his fingers. I was staring at the floor, but I could feel his gaze on me. My voice came out no more than a whisper.

"Where were you?"

"Luke's cousin was whipping up some drama and refused to let me go. I'm sorry I took so long," he said.

"So you weren't flirting with another girl?"

He sounded surprised. "No, of course not. I was trying to get rid of one."

It was difficult to speak past the enormous lump in my throat. I knew I was going to do something that I was going to regret, but I needed an answer. I didn't want to get jealous, or get hurt, or feel all these emotions for someone who might not like me back. Maybe if I heard him say it with his own mouth, then I'd stop liking him. And since I couldn't do it sober, why not do it now?

I mustered up the courage to say the four words.

"Do you like me?"

★* Y.O.L.O - I.J Hidee ★*

Chapter 22: A Good Guy

Killian blinked in surprise. It took him a few seconds to process my question. His eyebrows pulled together, and his jaw tightened slightly. The silence that followed felt like an eternity, and within those few seconds, I felt a jumble of emotions: fear, regret, excitement, hope...

But my heart dropped when Killian shifted his gaze. My cheeks flushed with heat and my stomach went heavy. I couldn't help but feel embarrassed by my ridiculous question. What was I thinking? Killian and I were too different. I followed the rules; he broke them. Water didn't mix with oil.

But for some ridiculous reason, I didn't want to give up either. Maybe it was the alcohol, or the drugs, or the simple desire of wanting him, but I stood up and kissed him. That's right, my first kiss.

Wait, was this considered sexual assault?

Killian pulled away slightly.

"You're supposed to move your lips, silly," he whispered. He wrapped his arms around my thin waist, locking his hands behind my back as he lowered his head to my height, our lips meeting once more. It felt magical.

He opened my mouth with his. My eyes widened at the new feeling, having no idea what I was doing with my mouth, but Killian guided me with his tongue. The warmth of his lips spread to my entire body, igniting a sensation inside me I've never felt before.

Unlike me, he knew how to kiss, and I bet he knew himself how great of a kisser he was. My knees buckled, and I clutched onto his hard chest. His hands explored down my back, reaching my butt and giving it a tight squeeze. A moan escaped my lips.

"Do you want to do it?"

My eyes fluttered open, and I looked at him in surprise.

"It?" I asked. He looked away.

"Never mind, forget what I said," he replied briskly.

And then it hit me.

"Sex?" I blurted bluntly. "Are you asking me if I want to have sex?"

Killian chuckled awkwardly, but he wouldn't look me in the eyes.

"I was just joking," he said, trying to brush it off.

"Let's do it," I said eagerly. I wanted Killian, and I knew it wasn't because of the substances. He let out a ripple of laughter, but when he realized that I was being serious, his expression turned serious.

"You're drunk."

"I'm not," I said. He raised a brow. "I mean, yes, I am, but it isn't because of the alcohol."

Killian remained still, so I lied.

"I want to try something new. You said that I always follow the rules and never step out of my comfort zone." I took a step closer to him. "Well, here I am, stepping out of my comfort zone."

"You're going to regret it."

"We only live once, right?" I chuckled nervously. Killian was silent for a moment. He lowered his gaze to mine.

"I'm not going to be gentle with you," he warned me. The look in his eyes both scared and excited me.

"Do you still want to do it?" he asked one last time. He was giving me a last chance out, but I didn't take it.

"I do," I said boldly.

My heart raced inside my chest and my cheeks flushed red. He leaned closer and I closed my eyes, waiting for his lips to touch mine. But they never did. His head fell on my shoulder, and he groaned.

"We can't," he muttered. "Not like this."

★* Y.O.L.O - I.J Hidee ★*

My heart dropped.

"What do you mean?" I asked weakly. He pulled away, creating a distance between us, but it now felt like he was out of my reach.

"Jones, you've been drugged and not to mention, completely drunk. I can't take advantage of you. Besides, you're still a—" he didn't finish his sentence, but I felt ashamed. "I'm sorry, I just can't. I'll wait for you outside."

He left before I could say anything.

***

The ride home was quiet and awkward, a dangerous combo. Killian told me if I felt sick, he could stop the car. I felt stick to my stomach, but even if I had a bullet in my chest, I wouldn't ask him to stop. I wanted to get home as soon as possible.

I swore to myself that I'd never go to a party again. It was a mistake. I was drunk, drugged, embarrassed, and worst of all, heartbroken. All in all, I was a complete mess. We arrived at my neighborhood and Killian parked his jeep in front of my house. I stiffened when I saw him reach for the door handle.

"You don't need to walk me to the door," I said, stopping him. He frowned but didn't insist.

"Are you going to be okay?" he asked worriedly. Okay was the last thing I was going to be, but I nodded.

"Why wouldn't I?" I laughed emptily.

"Your parents are pretty strict."

I felt a stab in the chest. The fact that Killian was pretending like he didn't know only made things worse.

"I'll be fine," I answered coldly.

"If you need anything, give me a call." He paused, raking a hand through his hair. I could tell he regretted those words. "Right, I forgot you can't call on the weekdays. If you need anything, send me a text."

"Bye." I stumbled out of his car and slammed the door shut.

"Jones," he called. I turned around and our gazes locked. I felt a spark of hope flicker inside my chest.

"Don't worry about what happened. It wasn't your fault."

And my hope came crashing to the ground, burning in flames. I knew exactly what he was thinking — Jones was drunk not thinking clearly. But he was wrong.

I kissed him because I wanted to. I would have slept with him because I wanted to. I liked Killian before I was drunk and drugged, and I liked him still after.

I swallowed the lump in my throat.

"You're right, I wasn't being myself," I said, but my voice came out broken. "So can you do me a favor and forget what happened?"

His lips pressed into a firm line, but he nodded.

"Of course."

I forced a smile.

"Then I'll see you whenever you come back to school!" I said, turning on my heel before dropping the smile. Tears poured down my cheeks like a waterfall. I could hear him start the engines and when I looked over my shoulder, he was already gone. The neighborhood fell silent, and I've never felt more alone than I did now.

★* Y.O.L.O - I.J Hidee ★*

Chapter 23: An Unhealthy Relationship

I wiped away the last of my tears and fanned my face before going inside. The second I opened the door, my parents stormed out of the living room with furious looks in their eyes.

"Carter Jones, where were you?!" Mom demanded.

"Why didn't you answer any of our calls?" Dad asked angrily, shaking his phone in his hand. I was terrified of Mom, but it was hard to take my dad seriously when he was wearing polka dot pajamas and fluffy shark slippers.

Mom sniffed the air and gave me a bewildered look.

"Did you drink?" She squinted her eyes and studied my face. "Carter, are you drunk?"

I didn't answer and she let out a cry of despair, putting the back of her hand on her forehead.

"Oh goodness," she gasped, fainting in my dad's arms. "Oh, Saint Mary, what happened to our son?"

★* Y.O.L.O - I.J Hidee ★*

He got his heartbroken.

"You have a lot of explaining to do, young man," Dad said. "We did not raise you to become a drunkard on the streets."

The normal Carter would have stood there, ashamed. The normal Carter would have apologized over and over again until he was forgiven. The normal Carter would have let himself be pushed around. But I was fed up. I was tired of being good, tired of my parents, tired of liking someone who didn't like me back, and tired of living this miserable life.

'It's your life.'

I giggled at the ridiculous thought. No, I burst into laughter, clutching my stomach and bending forward. I probably looked crazy. But reality whirled back into place when I heard a loud slap. It took a few seconds for me to realize that my mom had slapped me. I touched the side of my cheek and flinched at the stinging pain. Mom looked surprised herself and I could see regret pool in her eyes, but she didn't apologize. I took in a shaky breath.

"Thank you for controlling my life and making it a living hell, Mom and Dad, you guys are the best."

They stared at me, shocked. I stormed into my room and slammed the door shot, plopping onto my bed and sobbing into my pillow. The rest of the world became a blur.

***

★* Y.O.L.O - I.J Hidee ★*

My parents confiscated my phone, and I wasn't allowed to leave the house. We didn't talk about what happened that night. Eshe saw me at my lockers and greeted me with a smile.

"Carty!" She beamed. When I turned towards her, her eyes widened. "What happened?"

My eyes were puffy from crying all night.

"I didn't get much sleep."

"Were you up studying?"

Her question depressed me.

"No, I was sick."

I spent most of the night making trips to the bathroom, puking my guts out. My throat was sore, and my stomach still hadn't recovered. Eshe studied my face, then said, "It was Killian, wasn't it? What did he do this time? Carter, I told you—"

"You were right," I said flatly.

"Why won't you listen— Wait, what?"

"You were right. I got hurt," I said with a sad smile. Eshe's eyebrows pulled together and her lips slightly parted.

"Can we not talk about it?" My voice must have came out desperate, because Eshe pursed her lips and nodded.

"Okay," Eshe said, clasping my hand and giving it a gentle squeeze. "We don't have to talk about it. But just so you know, whatever he did, I'm going to make him pay for it."

A small smile cracked on my face.

"Ugh, I smell losers," we heard someone say. Desiree walked down the halls in her new pink pumps. She held a designer purse instead of a backpack and stabbed us with a nasty glare.

"And I smell a bitch," Eshe retorted.

"Nerd," Desiree shot back.

"Hoe."

Desiree flicked her middle finger and Eshe stuck out her tongue. When Desiree was gone, Eshe slammed my locker shut.

"Ugh, I hate her so much," she growled in irritation.

"You rarely hate people."

"Yeah, but she's an exception." She then cleared her voice. "Anyway, what are you doing after school? Detention?"

The thought of having detention with Killian made me frown. I nodded.

"You're going to be careful, right?" she asked slowly.

"I always am."

★* Y.O.L.O - I.J Hidee ★*

The bell rang and we headed to class. We took our seats and prepared for our science test. I went through my notes when the teacher did roll call and didn't put stop revising until the teacher told us to put everything in our bags. We weren't allowed to have anything other than a sheet of paper and our pencil cases on our desks. The teacher was handing out the papers when the door suddenly opened.

Our eyes widened in surprise.

Killian didn't ask if he could come in, nor did he apologize for being late. He simply sat down and took out his pencil case. Gasps and murmurs filled the room. Even our teacher seemed shocked to see him, but he wasn't going to kick him out for coming to class.

Was it me or was Killian sitting closer to the front? He normally sat at the very back. Killian looked over his shoulder and before I could look away, his gaze met mine. My chest tightened.

He winked and flashed me a smile. I quickly lowered my gaze, feeling my cheeks turn red.

The test started and I pushed away my thoughts. I wish I could do the same with my feelings.

★* Y.O.L.O - I.J Hidee ★*

Chapter 24: Casper the Friendly Ghost

I went to the library to borrow a chemistry book. I scanned the shelves and found the book I was looking for. I had to stand on my toes to reach for it, but my fingers didn't reach the spine. I winced as I stretched my arm further.

Just a little more...

But someone pulled out the book for me. My first thought was Killian, but then I remembered that the library was probably foreign territory to him. I turned around and blinked in confusion. Standing behind me was a tall boy with long brown hair. He had a nice sunny smile that matched his nice warm eyes.

"Here," he said, handing me the book.

"Thank you," I answered in a daze. I waited for him to leave, but he didn't.

"Carter, right?" he prompted. I nodded, slightly confused.

"How do you know my name?"

"I saw you busting out some sick moves at the party. It was pretty lit," he chuckled, suddenly doing the sprinkler. My mouth dropped open and I quickly lowered his arms to his sides, frantically looking around us to make sure no one saw.

"Please don't do that," I begged. Everything from that night needed to be burned from my memoires.

The boy chuckled, looking down at my hands that were still on his arms. I quickly let go and took a step back, bumping into the self behind me and wincing in pain.

"Ouch," I mumbled. Casper chuckled, but not in a mean way.

"Oh right, I forgot to introduce myself. I'm Casper."

Like Casper the friendly ghost.

He raised a brow. "Uh yeah, like him."

I mentally groaned when I realized that I had said my thoughts aloud again. I needed to fix this bad habit of mine.

"Sorry," I murmured sheepishly. "It's just that I really liked watching that show when I was little. I used to dress up as him for Halloween, and-"

I stopped and bit my tongue. Be quiet, Carter! Stop embarrassing yourself!

I quickly cleared my voice.

"So, er, yeah," I concluded miserably with a weak smile.

"I used to watch that show all the time too," Casper beamed. "That stuff's old school. I didn't think anyone would remember it. Then again, you did bust out the sprinkler the other day," he chuckled, starting to dance again. I quickly stopped him but couldn't help but laugh with him.

"That's not funny," I said, trying to sound serious but failing terribly. We were hushed by some of the students who were trying to study. Casper and I shared a look and we giggled as quietly as we could.

"We should probably leave. Do you have class?" he asked as we headed out the library.

"I have detention."

He raised his eyebrows.

"Detention? You don't look like someone who'd get detention."

"I'm not. Well, I wasn't," I said sheepishly. Casper opened the door for me, and I thanked him.

"Oh, hey, you have something stuck in your hair," he noted. I patted my head.

"Where? Here?"

"A little to the left," he informed me. I moved my hand and brushed my hair with my fingers.

"Is it gone?"

"No, a little bit more to the left," he said as I continued to pat around. "No, no, a bit more to the right."

"How about now?"

"Here, I'll get it for you," he said, extending his hand.

"Jones?" Said a voice. We turned to the side and my eyes widened as I saw Killian. I stepped away from Casper as if I was caught doing something bad.

"You've got something in your hair," he said, reaching over and removing the fluff.

He blew the cotton from his fingertip and flashed me a smile. Why did everything he do have to be so attractive?!

"All better," he beamed.

"What are you doing here?" I frowned.

"I came to look for you, why else?"

"Killian, right?" Casper said, breaking our gaze. Killian smiled at him politely, but there was something off about it.

"Yeah, that's me."

Casper extended his hand. "My name is—"

"Annoying," Killian interrupted. Casper and I looked at him in surprise and Killian suddenly waved his hand in the air. "There's an annoying fly in the air."

His eyes then focused on Casper. "Oh, you were saying?"

Casper lowered his hand and shoved it into his pocket. His eyes looked less eager.

"Casper," he said. "My name is Casper."

Killian turned towards me and his warm smiled returned.

"We should go, or we'll be late for detention."

Killian? Being punctual? Someone pinch me.

"Since when did you care about being on time?" I asked suspiciously.

"Since Mr. Thirdwheel here tried to touch your hair," he said. "I'm kidding," he chuckled dryly. "Now let's go, I don't remember which room we're in."

He took my hand and pulled me down the corridors. I looked over my shoulder.

"It was nice meeting you!" I waved at Casper, sad that I had to leave so soon.

"Yeah, same here. Maybe we can hang out and watch Casper the Friendly Ghost together."

"Yeah, I'd like that," I beamed.

Killian let go of me only when Casper was no longer in sight.

"What the fuck is Casper the friendly ghost?" He growled bitterly, the tone of his voice making me even more confused.

"You don't have to swear," I murmured. "It was my favorite show when I was a kid."

Killian remained quiet. Did something bad happen to him this morning? Did he fight with Luke? Or maybe Francisco? I wanted to ask him but reminded myself that I needed to distance myself from him. Asking him would mean that I cared, and I didn't want to care.

We made it to detention, but he stopped.

"Jones," he said in a formal tone. I turned towards him.

"Killian," I replied.

"I'm sorry."

My brows quirked.

"For swearing?" I laughed gently. "It's okay, Killian. You don't need to apologize."

"No, not that. I mean yes, that too," he grumbled. "I was talking about Saturday."

My smile vanished. "Oh."

"I know you asked me to forget about it, but I can't."

"We should go in. Mr. Yon is probably waiting for us."

I tried to open the door, but Killian side-stepped.

"I know you don't want to talk about it but hear me out. I shouldn't have left you with Jenna. No, I shouldn't have left you at all, not when I promised to look after you. I know this sounds like a cra— I mean, lame excuse." He was trying to keep his vocabulary PG-13. "But I thought I could trust her. I'm sorry."

He looked at me with genuine eyes and poured his heart into each word.

"It's okay, Killian, I'm not upset. And I'm sorry too."

He stared at me blankly. "For what?"

"For sexually harassing you."

He coughed. "Sexually harassing me?"

"I kissed you without asking first," I reminded him. Killian blinked then burst into laughter.

"I'm serious!" I frowned.

"Sorry, you're just too cute," he said, wiping away a tear. I crossed my arms over my chest with narrowed eyes.

No, sir, I was not cute. I was smoking hot. Like a potato. A smoking hot potato. A really piping hot— Okay, I should stop now.

"Jones, I didn't mind the kiss. You were terrible at it, but I didn't mind."

My mouth dropped open. *Terrible?!*

"It was my first time!" I protested defensively. Killian stared at me, and I realized the mistake I made.

"Uh, I mean, um—" It wasn't even worth denying. "We have detention."

"Was I really your first?" He asked, his eyes free of judgement.

I dug my own grave, now I must lie in it. "Maybe."

His head hung and he let out a small groan.

"Shit, sorry."

"Why are you apologizing?"

"I dunno, you seem like the type of person who would treasure his first kiss. I feel like I ruined something that should have been special to you."

It was special. It was special because it was with you.

"You aren't mad at me, are you?" he asked, his eyes clouding with worry. I shook my head.

"No, are you?"

It was the first time I saw Killian smile today. A real one.

"No," he answered. "How could I ever be mad at you?"

Chapter 25: Y.O.L.O

"Do you want to go somewhere after detention?" Killian asked suddenly. I looked up from my notes.

"Is this another dare?"

"Not everything has to be a dare, Jones," he chuckled. I bit my lower lip. I knew I shouldn't, but I couldn't help but ask.

"Where do you want to go?"

"You'll see," he beamed.

Killian rarely told me where we went, but I guess that that was what made things exciting. It made me realize how much I've changed since I've met him. I normally would have declined his offer or would have squirmed at the thought of not knowing where we were going. Now? Now the unknown excited me. And I trusted Killian. Even though he had left me at the party, I knew he never meant to hurt me. There was a difference between being a bad person and making a mistake.

★* Y.O.L.O - I.J Hidee ★*

We hopped into his jeep and drove down the road. He didn't ask me any questions or force a conversation, which I appreciated. I guess that that was his way of acknowledging what had happened at the party without actually acknowledging it. I wondered if things were ever be the same between us.

"Do you want some gum?" he suddenly asked, opening the center console.

"Um, no thank you."

He nodded and popped three into his mouth. The muscles in his jaw worked as he chewed, and I couldn't tear my eyes away.

Why did he offer me gum? Did my breath stink? Or was he getting ready to kiss me? I suddenly found myself getting anxious.

"It's a good replacement for the cigarettes," he said, snapping me out of my thoughts.

"What happened to the lollipops?"

He shrugged. "Decided I needed a change."

I pressed my lips into a smile, glad that he hadn't smoked yet. "I'm glad you didn't break your promise."

"Promises are meant to be broken." His green eyes flickered towards me, and he flashed me a smile. "But I'll try my best to keep my word with you."

We got further away from the city.

"Is this the part where you murder me and hide my corpse in the woods?" I asked, starting to get nervous. He grinned.

"Caught me red-handed. Welp, I guess it's time to dump your body—"

My head snapped towards him. "Killian!"

"I'm kidding," he chuckled. A flicker of a smile again. I sank in my seat, trying to ignore the feeling inside my chest. Killian slowed down and parked his car.

"Hiking?" I asked.

"Hiking," he confirmed.

My eyebrows scrunched but I followed him out his jeep. We climbed up the steep forest, but the path was bumpy and poorly paved. Killian didn't have a hard time going up and moved swiftly like he's walked this track a hundred times. I kept slipping and tripping over rocks. I was falling behind and ran to catch up to him, but I yelped when my ankle got caught in a fallen branch.

"Ouch," I mumbled, picking myself up.

"You okay?" Killian asked.

"Yeah," I lied. He pursed his lips.

"Here," he said, giving his hand. I stared at it. He read the expression on my face and said, "Just until we reach the top."

I bit my lower lip but took his hand. Mine were sweaty, and I was about to ask him if it bothered him, but he gave me a gentle squeeze just like the first time we held hands.
The cold metal of his rings contrasted with the warmth of his skin, and the size difference between his hand and mine was jarring — but it felt right. Something about the way our hands fitted felt terribly right.

I didn't understand what kind of relationship Killian and I had anymore. We weren't just classmates or friends or boyfriend and boyfriend. We gave each other dares, went on adventures, and occasionally held hands.

We reached the top and he stopped at a large tree. I knew what he was thinking.

"I can't climb up there," I said.

"I'll help you."

Killian swiftly pulled himself up. He gave out his hand and helped me climb up the tree. We went to the highest branch and sat down. My eyes widened at the scenery. The sky was pastel pink with swirls of orange and splashes of red. You could see the never-ending treetops from here. It was like a forest of broccoli.

"I used to come up here when I was a kid," Killian said. "It's nice, don't you think?"

My eyes widened when I realized that I recognized this place from the photo his mom gave me. It was the same branch under the same sky. Except Killian was no longer a little boy. I glanced at his profile. His features were strong and defined, and his jaw was sharp. The brilliant green in his eyes remained the same though, framed in long dark lashes. The late noon sunlight kissed his olive skin.

"Ask me something," Killian said softly, and I snapped my head straight ahead. I hope he didn't catch me staring.

"What do you want me to ask?"

"Anything but that," he winked.

I pursed my lips, deep in thought, then said, "Why don't you like commitment?"

He pressed his hands against the branch and leaned back as he stared at the sky. Killian didn't answer for a moment, lost in his thoughts.

"I don't want to be like my dad."

His answer caught me by surprise, and I knitted my eyebrows.

"Commitment means responsibilities and responsibilities means expectations. If you fail any one of them, then you end up hurting someone. I don't want to hurt people, especially those I love." My eyes widened at his candor. "I don't want to hurt someone the way my dad hurt my mom. I guess I don't like commitment because I'm scared."

He ran a hand through his hair, then let out a nervous chuckle as if his answer surprised him too. His eyes flickered towards me.

"Are you disappointed that I'm not as cool and fearless as you thought?" He asked.

"I like this side of you," I said in a heartbeat. He tilted his head back and laughed the most beautiful melody I've heard.

"Then let's keep it between us."

Us.

My heart fluttered, but I managed to nod. Killian had a way with his words that I couldn't quite explain. I felt special, like I was the only one in the world.

It was only when he pulled away that I noticed we'd been holding hands the entire time. I felt a gentle breeze kiss my palm and my hand felt empty without his.

"Now it's my turn," he said.

""Your turn?"

"To ask a question."

Was that why he asked me to ask him a question? He was so sly, I wasn't even mad.

"What do you want to know?" I asked nervously.

"Who slapped you?" The change of tone surprised me. "I want a name and address."

I stared at him, my mouth hanging open.

"You're not planning on murdering the person, are you?" I said jokingly. He raised a shoulder.

"Well, I know a guy— "

"Killian!"

"I'm kidding," he said, then grumbled. "Kind of."

"Killian, you are not murdering my mom," I snapped.

His eyebrows shot up.

"Your Mom slapped you?"

I nodded. "How did you know?"

"Your left cheek is slightly redder than your right."

"It's hardly noticeable," I frowned. Even Eshe who sat right beside me in class didn't notice.

"It is if you pay attention."

I looked away to hide the blush blooming on my cheeks. If they weren't the same color before, they were now.

"I got in a fight with my parents after the party. I talked back to them for the first time and my mom lost her temper. She didn't mean to slap me. It just sort of happened."

"Wait, you talked back to your parents?"

"Um, yes?"

"Jones, that's amazing!" he exclaimed.

"What?"

Killian put his hands on my shoulders and shook me gently.

"Mr. Goodie-two-shoes talked back to his parents; can you believe that? I'm so proud of you!" he beamed, pulling me in and hugging me tightly. I could feel my chest pound against his. "Carter Jones has finally spoken up."

"But I got slapped," I frowned.

"That's called bad parenting, it has nothing to do with you," he said dismissively. "You've spent your entire life living a safe and secure life, but you've finally taken a risk. If that's not an accomplishment, then I don't know what is."

His hand fell from my shoulder, but I didn't want him to pull away, so I mustered up the courage to hold his hand. It was the first time I made a move, and I felt a wash of relief when he didn't pull away. I traced my thumb over his tattooed knuckles.

"What do you think I should do?" I asked. "I've never fought with my parents. At least, not like this."

"There's only one way to solve things."

"Which is?"

Killian pulled out something from his wallet and placed it in my hand. My eyebrows knitted in confusion.

"Go here and say whatever the fuck you want. Every secret, every complaint, every built of feeling that you've kept from your parents. And if you can't find the courage to do it, then tell yourself this. Act like today is your last day alive. There are some secrets you don't want to take to the grave, right? If you don't do it now, then you'll never have the chance to do it again. And if you still can't do it, then tell yourself that no matter what happens, it was worth it."

His words hit harder than I expected, and I felt a lump in my throat. I wish Killian knew how much he meant to me. Not just as a crush, but as a person. I wish he knew how much I admired him, and how much he's changed my life.

A boy with a silly acronym tattooed on his knuckles on a quest to find the meaning behind living once had taught me one of the biggest life lessons anyone could have taught me.

Stop existing. Start living.

★* Y.O.L.O - I.J Hidee ★*

Chapter 26: If Today Were My Last

My parents and I sat down in front of the lady.

"So, tell me why you're here," the therapist smiled politely.

This was the place Killian told me to go. He had given me a therapist's business card. Why he had one or where he got it, I had no idea. I never thought that my crush would tell me to go see a therapist with my parents. Then again, this boy was always full of surprises.

Dad cleared his voice.

"Our son thought that it would be a good idea to see a professional and talk about our... Problems," he said.

The therapist nodded.

"Don't worry, Mr. Jones, many parents come to my office with their teenagers. It's normal for children their age to have behavioral problems," she reassured him. My eyebrows pulled together. I don't think I was the one with behavioral problems.

The therapist turned towards me, and I stiffened.

"What's your name?" she asked.

"Carter Jones."

"Can you tell me why you're here?"

"My mom slapped me," I said bluntly, and realized how bad that sounded. But the therapist kept a neutral face and nodded, scribbling something down in her notes before turning towards Mom.

"Mrs. Jones, can you tell me why you hit your son?"

Mom flinched.

"I was upset," she said hastily.

"Violence is never the answer," the therapist said.

"It didn't hurt," I said in Mom's defense. "It would have been worse if Dad hit me."

The three adults turned towards me with strange looks on their faces. I let out a nervous chuckle and squeezed my hands between my thighs. The therapist was the first to break the silence.

"From my observations, Carter, you seem to think that whatever they do is okay because their adults, but adults make mistakes too," Mrs. Browne said. "Age is important, but it doesn't excuse everything."

I blinked in surprise.

"Think about it this way. What if you were the one who slapped your mom? How would you feel if she said, 'It's okay, it didn't hurt that much anyway. He's my son."

I stiffened.

"Now put yourself in a third person's view. What would you do if your friend told you that they've been slapped by their parents?"

I frowned. "I'd call the police."

She nodded.

"There are two types of abuse," the therapist said. "Physical and emotional. Just because you can't see the second one doesn't mean it doesn't exist. Have your parents put you through any emotional hardships?"

My parents looked at me with frowns on their faces. I felt pressured not to say anything, but I remembered what Killian told me. I took in a tight breath.

"I think so, yes," I finally said.

"You think or you know? You have to be sure, Carter."

"I have," I said.

"Wait, we—"

Mrs. Browne cut my mom off with a hand.

"Mrs. Jones, please. I'm speaking with your son," she said sharply. Mom's jaw tightened, but she remained still. Mrs. Browne turned towards me.

"Is there anything you'd like to tell your parents?" she asked.

'Act like today is your last day alive. There are some secrets you don't want to take to the grave, right? If you don't do it now, then you'll never have the chance to do it again. And if you still can't do it, then tell yourself that no matter what happens, it was worth it.'

There were a million things I wanted to say. Perhaps I should start with the easiest. I took in a deep breath, tightened my fists, and looked at my parents.

"Mom, Dad," I said. "I'm gay."

Their eyes shot open in surprise.

"I don't like Eshe because I don't like girls, and I hope you'll stop pressuring me to like her because I don't. At least, not in that way. I like boys. Even though I'm a boy, I like guys, and I hope you'll accept the way I am."

Mom bit her lower lip, but to my surprise, she nodded. She didn't yell at me or tell me I was wrong. She listened, and so did Dad.

"And I hope you'll stop controlling my life. I feel like I've wasted so much time trying to live up to your expectations that I forgot that this was my life. When I think about all the friends I could have had, the experiences I could have made, the memories I could have built, I feel sad. I feel sad because those are past tenses that never happened because you didn't want that for me. But I did," I said. "And I'm going to have to live with those regrets for the rest of my life."

The room went silent. Then my mom burst into tears. She got up from her seat and hugged me, apologizing between sobs. I felt a lump in my throat and swallowed hard. When I looked down, a tear dribbled off my chin, and I realized that I was crying too. Dad stood up and gently tousled my hair. He didn't say a word, but the look in his eyes was enough to tell me that he was sorry.

Even though I couldn't change the past, I could change the future. *My* future. It was my life, and it was time I lived it that way. No matter how we lived, we were all going to die one day. We might as well live life to the fullest.

It was the risks I took like today that I'd one day look back at and think to myself, *you only live once, Carter, but once is enough.*

★* Y.O.L.O - I.J Hidee ★*

Chapter 27: Crossdressing

I had the feeling that Killian was avoiding me. He didn't make it noticeable enough for me to ask him about it, but enough for me to know.

He came to class and greeted me whenever he saw me in the hallways. We chatted in detention, but the conversations never lasted very long. He didn't mention our bet either. He was slowly distancing himself from me, and I didn't understand why. I thought liking Killian made me miserable. Turns out, not having him in my life only made it worse.

I wanted to tell him that the therapy session went well and that my parents and I were working things out. I also wanted to tell him how amazing Mrs. Browne was.

And then one day, I got a call from him.

"Your fourth and last dare," was the first thing he said. "I need you to help me break someone out of jail."

"What?"

"My best friend Francisco got into a fight near a grocery store with some kids at his school. He's at the police station behind bars. We'll take my jeep and get him out of jail."

"Wait, we?" I asked, still trying to process what he was saying. "Shouldn't his parents be the ones picking him up?"

"We'll go in disguised as his parents. I'll be the dad, you can be his mom."

It was official. Killian had completely lost his mind. I took in a steady breath.

"Killian, I don't know if you're aware, but I am a boy! How am I supposed act as his mom when I'm a guy?!"

"You're thin, frail-looking, and have a snatched waist. Throw on a wig, put on some make-up, and voilà, you have a girl."

I didn't know if I should be flattered or offended.

"And I'll be there acting as your lovely husband. There's nothing to worry about."

There was everything to worry about! His plan could go wrong in so many ways, starting from his idea!

"Impersonating another person is against the law," I said sternly.

"All we have to do is sign some papers and get him out of jail, easy peasy lemon squeezy."
"Killian, are you out of your mind?!"

"There's a high chance, yes."

I squeezed my temples and scrunched my eyebrows.

"Killian, this isn't what I'd call Y.O.L.O. This is 'top ten ways to get yourself in jail!"

"You're overthinking."

"Yes, but at least I'm thinking."

"C'mon, Jones, I'll be with you. I promise I won't let anything happen to you this time." When I didn't answer, he said, "Look, I wouldn't be asking you if I wasn't desperate. Francis is my best friend. He's like a brother to me. I can't leave him in there."

When I didn't answer, he said, "This is the last dare. Please, Jones, I can't do this without you."

I hated myself for giving in.

"Alright, fine," I mumbled.

"Perfect. Meet me at my house. We have a crime to commit."

***

Killian laid out a handful of make-up on the table. I picked one up and squinted my eyes.

"Channel," I read.

"I think that's pronounced sha-nnel (Chanel)," Killian chuckled. I picked another one up.

"Dire," I read aloud.

"Um, that's probably Dee-or (Dior)," he noted. I then grabbed another one, furrowing my eyebrows in confusion. "Who's Sephora?"

"Alright, you're more lost than I am," he said, taking the makeup out of my hands. "We'll need to ask Uncle Google for help."

Killian did some research on his laptop.

"Alright, do you want to go for a natural look or a heavy, smokey one?"

"Maybe the more natural one?"

"Good choice."

"Wait, but do you know how to use any of these?"

"Nope," he smiled proudly. "Not a clue."

We sat on the floor, and he began applying makeup on my face. I wanted to ask him why he's been avoiding me, but he was so focused on putting on my makeup that I didn't want to bother him. While Killian worked on my face, I spent the hour admiring his beautiful face.

"Here, put this on," he said, handing me a wig. He helped me adjust it on my head.

"Do I look weird?" I asked worriedly. He blinked in surprise.

"No, you look beautiful," he promised. He said it with so much conviction that I believed him. He handed me a mirror. "What do you think?"

My eyes widened when I saw myself. I could hardly recognize myself. The makeup wasn't too heavy or cakey. Killian had perfected the natural makeup look. The mascara extended my lashes and brought out my eyes, and the shades of contour gave the illusion of a more feminine face. I was shocked. No, I was *amazed*. I really did look like a girl.

"You did amazing."

"Ah, you're making me blush. Oh, and here."

He handed me some clothes. A blouse and a skirt.

"They belong to my mom, but she doesn't wear them anymore."

I nodded but felt my cheeks redden when I remembered the last time I changed in front of him. I awkwardly averted his gaze.

"Can I change in the bathroom?" I asked shyly.

"Oh, uh, yeah, of course. It's down the hall," he said. Was it me or did he sound disappointed? Probably just me. I thanked him and went to change. I put on the blue blouse and skirt. It felt breezy in the lower hemisphere.

When I went back to Killian's room, he was standing shirtless in front of his closet. I sucked in a tight breath as I watched him pull a sweater over his head, his back and arm muscles moving in harmony. He looked over his shoulder and I blushed.

"Oh, I didn't see you there," he said casually.

"What do you think?" I asked, stepping into the room to show him the look. He walked towards me, gently tucking a lock of hair behind my ear. He stood so close, it reminded me of the night we kissed. Heat instantly flared through my cheeks. It was too obvious for him not to notice.

"Like I said," he murmured in a husky voice. "You look beautiful."

Even though he had probably said that to dozens of girls, it was the first time anyone has said that to me. My heart hammered wildly against my chest, I was scared he might hear it. It was hard not to blush when someone looked at you the way Killian did.

I like you so much, I think I'm going crazy.

Killian took a step back, his eyebrows slowly gathering.

"What?"

The blood in my face drained down my neck, and I knew I was doomed.

★* Y.O.L.O - I.J Hidee ★*

Chapter 28: Husband and Wife

Killian drove down the road. There was an awkward silence that hung between us, the kind of silence that made you wish you never existed. I stared out the window, drowning in regret. I had accidentally confessed to Killian. Who accidentally confesses to their crush?!

"Do you want to listen to some music?" Killian asked, breaking the silence. He didn't wait for me to answer and turned on the radio.

Crazy in Love by Beyoncé started playing. My body stiffened at the lyrics.

Got me looking so crazy right now, your love's,
Got me looking so crazy right now,
Got me looking so crazy right now,
Got me hoping you'll-

I quickly changed the station.

The Crush Song by Twaimz started playing.

Hush, hush, hush
Blush, blush, blush

★* Y.O.L.O - I.J Hidee ★*

You are now my big fat crush
I'm single as I can be
You're single, perfect for me
I'm gonna give you a bunch of reasons
Why you should date me
Reason number one - I'm super hot
Reason number two - she's super not
Reason number three - I'm all you got
And all you got is someone hot-

My face reddened and I changed the station again, praying that it wouldn't be a love song.

I mentally groaned when Love you like a love song by Selena Gomez started playing.

I, I love you like a love song, baby
I, I love you like a love song, baby
I, I love you like a love song, baby
And I keep it in re-pe-pe-peat

Killian shut off the radio, and I closed my eyes, trying not to die inside.

We didn't talk for the rest of the ride. He parked in front of a grocery store not too far from the police station.

"Can we talk about what happened earlier?" Killian asked. My stomach went rigid and I opened the car door, but Killian caught my arm.

"Are you mad at me?" he asked worriedly. I knew he wanted me to look him in the eyes, but I couldn't.

"No, I'm not mad at you," I murmured.

★* Y.O.L.O - I.J Hidee ★*

"Upset?"

"No."

"Sad?"

"N—"

"Depressed?"

"Your friend is in jail," I tried to remind him.

"So we're just going to ignore what happened?" he asked, now frustrated.

My lips pressed together. He was right. We couldn't keep pretending like nothing happened between us. I turned towards him, opened my mouth, but nothing would come out. In my mind, I could imagine myself telling him how I felt, but when I looked into Killian's emerald eyes, I froze. The words were lodged in my throat. I was scared. No, I was *terrified*.

You're a chicken, Carter, a scolding voice said in my mind.

But confronting my crush had to be ten times scarier than confronting my parents. My pulse raced and my mind went into a panicking frenzy.

I was a chicken, perhaps, but a chicken who didn't want to get hurt.

I opened the door and got out of the jeep so quickly I almost fell. I smoothed my skirt and fixed my wig, walking with what dignity I had left. I could hear Killian's light footsteps from behind and before I knew it, he was beside me. We left the parking lot and walked down the busy streets. When we arrived at the police station, a new wave of fear hit me.

"We should hold hands." Killian spoke in a reasonable tone, but it was distant and slightly cold. "It'll make us look like a married couple. I mean, we did just have our first quarrel, didn't we?"

When I didn't answer, he gave out his hand.

"May I?"

I nodded and he gently took my hand. We entered the police station together and went to the front desk.

"Hello, how may I help you?" the lady asked. Her blue uniform intimidated me, and my hand tightened around Killian's. I tried to speak, but my voice was too dry, and I didn't know what to say. I looked at Killian who remained perfectly calm.

"We're looking for our son, Francisco Kohl," he said. The lady nodded and typed something into her computer.

"Your son has quite the criminal record," she said, scrolling down. "He got into another fight."

"Did he win?"

The lady glanced up. "Excuse me?"

"I said I'm going to have a word with him," Killian said, shaking his head.

★* Y.O.L.O - I.J Hidee ★*

"Your son is in cell 140, but I'll need to see your ID's first."

My body went stiff.

"My wife forgot hers. Is mine enough?" he asked smoothly, working his magic.

"Of course," she said. He took out his wallet and handed her his fake ID. I caught a glimpse.

Braxton Kohl, CEO, married, 52 years old.

"Aw, you two adopted Francisco? That's so sweet," she said.

"Raised him as our own."

"All you need to do is sign here and here," she said. We signed the papers, and she took us to his cell. Killian leaned towards me, his lips brushing against my ear.

"See? Easy peasy lemon squeezy," he whispered, low enough for only me to hear.

A handsome Asian boy was laying on a bed too small for him, listlessly throwing a tennis ball in the air. It was the same guy I saw standing in front of the school gates with Killian and Luke, except this time, he wasn't wearing a school uniform. He wore cargo pants and a black tank top that revealed his muscular arms and intimidating sleeve tattoo.
"Francisco, your parents are here to pick you up," said the lady, catching his attention. His eyes widened when he saw Killian.

"Kill— I mean Dad!" he exclaimed, jumping to his feet. The lady unlocked the door and he stepped out. He looked at me and squinted his eyes. "And er, mom?"

"Is that how you're going to greet your mom?" Killian snorted. "And jail? Really?"

Francisco let out a sheepish chuckle. "Yeah, sorry, won't happen again."

"That's what you always say," he grumbled. "Come on, let's go home."

"Oh, Mrs. Kohl, you have something in your hair," the lady said. My eyes widened, but before I could stop her, she pulled out whatever was caught in my hair, along with my wig. Her eyes went as wide as a saucepan.

"Dude, that lady just snatched Ma's wig," Francisco gasped.

"Run?" Killian gulped.

"Run," Francisco and I agreed.

"Hey, wait!" shouted the lady as we bolted down the hallway. We heard her yelling into her walkie-talkie. "I need backup in corridor 9, I repeat, I need backup in corridor 9. There are two boys and one girl on the loose."

I'm not a girl!
"I thought you said that everything was going to be fine!" I cried as we turned around the corner. Killian just laughed.

"I thought so too."

"Hey, who's the hot chick?" Francisco asked. He was worse than Killian.

"Oi, back off," growled Killian, pushing him away from me. "Go find your own wife."

"GUYS!" I shouted frantically.

I looked over my shoulder and my eyes widened at the number of policemen chasing us. Unlike these two giants, my body wasn't athletic or strong. They ran like cheetahs. I ran like a boy who didn't know how to run in a skirt. Killian noticed that I was falling behind and scooped me up, throwing me over his shoulder like a sack of potatoes as he continued to run with Francisco.

I clutched onto the back of his shirt, trying not to get sick as they ran out of the building. He put me down once when we made it to the bigger streets, but we didn't stop running.

"Come on, Carter, you're too slow!" Killian snickered. He gave me a gentle push forward, but I almost lost my balance. It was hard enough for me to run in a skirt, especially when I grew up only wearing pants.

"If you don't hurry, we'll get caught!"

He seemed too cheerful for someone being chased by five angry policemen. Killian wore a wide, confident grin and looked unbothered by the gravity of our situation. He looked like he was enjoying the thrill rather than fearing it.

Anyone could tell that this wasn't the first time committing a crime, nor was it his first getting caught. I found that both deeply worrisome and slightly reassuring.

Killian quickened his pace and ran ahead of me. The crowded streets became a hazy blur and all I could focus on was Killian's silhouette. I found myself once again enchanted by him. It was as if he was born to run. The wind brushed through his silky, dark hair, his strong arms pushed him forward, and his calves strengthened at each footfall. He looked free and full of life. A boy ready to conquer the world.

He looked over his shoulder, his bright pistachio-colored eyes glistening under the daylight. A smile grew at the corner of his lips, revealing his pearly white teeth. I wondered what toothpaste he used. Colgate? Crest? Elmex maybe?

"Carter," he said. "Take my hand."

He extended his arm, and I could see the acronym tattooed on his knuckles. Y.O.L.O.

"Well?" he laughed, snapping me out of my trance.

The wind knocked out my breath and a burning pain hurt my thighs, but I pushed myself to exceed my limits. I reached out and the tip of my fingers brushed against his. He grabbed my hand, our fingers intertwining.

Running side by side, we ran down the crowded streets, ignoring the shouts and stares, laughing and hooting like there was no tomorrow.

We finally made it to the parking lot. Before any of us could put on our seatbelts, Killian stepped on the pedal, and we zoomed out of there within seconds.

I tried to catch my breath, adrenaline pumping through my veins while Killian and Francisco high-fived each other, laughing their heads off. There had to be something seriously wrong with these boys.

"It's been a while Kiki," Francisco beamed. "I see you're still as reckless as ever."

"Says the guy who got himself in jail," Killian smirked. "I told you not to fight anymore."

"Ugh, you sound like Luke," he grumbled. He then turned towards me, and the cheerful smile returned on his face. His dark eyes sparkled with curiosity. "You still haven't introduced me to your pretty friend."

"He's not my friend," Killian grunted in a husky tone, pushing Francisco's face away from me. "He's my *wife*."

Chapter 29: Killian's Feelings

Francisco roared with laughter.

"Good one," he cackled, then his expression went serious. "No really, who is he?"

"I'm his classmate," I said shyly. "We have class together."

Francisco looked at Killian.

"Huh, I didn't know you went to school," he said, which made Killian roll his eyes.

"I go to school every now and then," Killian said. He then glanced at me with a smile dancing on the corner of his lips. "For Jones."

My eyes widened and I quickly averted his gaze.

"For detention," I corrected him so Francisco wouldn't get the wrong idea.

"Oh, wait, so you're Carter Jones?" Francisco gasped.

"You know me?"

"Yeah, Killian told me about you."

My brows shot up in surprise. "He did?"

"Yeah, he talks about you a lot. Seriously, like all the time."

"Francis, shut it," Killian snapped.

"What?" Francisco asked innocently. "I'm just trying to embarrass you."

I bit my lip trying not to smile. I couldn't believe that I ever thought Francisco was scary. He was a ball of sunshine.

"Does anyone have a cigarette? I've been dying for a smoke but apparently, smoking isn't allowed in jail. Ridiculous, I know!"

I gave him an apologetic smile. "Sorry, I don't smoke."

"It's fine," he said, then turned towards Killian who remained silent. Francisco poked his shoulder.

"C'mon Killian, don't be stingy," he cooed.

"I don't have any cigs," Killian replied coldly.

"Aw, don't be like that. I'll buy you some more later."

"I really don't have any."

"But you always have cigarettes," Francisco sulked.

"Well, not this time," he said. "I cut off on the cigs."

Francisco's jaw dropped wide open. He grabbed Killian, almost making us crash into the car next to us.

"Dude!" Killian hissed, pushing him away.

"Who are you and what did you do to my beloved Killian?!"

He turned towards me.

"Can you believe this? Killian Henderson said he cut off—" he didn't finish his sentence, taking in a deep breath. "Wow, you get stuck in jail for a day and the entire world just drastically changes before your eyes. The next thing you know, pigs are going to fly and unicorns are going to take over the world!"

I let out a stiff laugh. "Um, I'm the one who asked him to stop smoking."

Francisco's mouth widened again. I was scared his jaw might pop at this point.

"What happened while I was in jail?" he murmured weakly, looking from me to Killian. "Because this... None of this is making any sense."

"What doesn't make sense?" Killian sighed.

"Does one plus one equal three?"

"No?"

"Exactly!" Francisco cried, throwing his hands in the air.

I giggled.

"Look, just suck on this if you're so desperate for a smoke," Killian said, throwing a lollipop to his friend. Francisco shrugged, unwrapping it and happily popping it into his mouth. "So where do I drop you off? Your house or Luke's?"

"Ugh, not that brat's house," Francisco groaned.

"Luke?" I asked.

"Yeah, they're dating," Killian informed me. My eyes widened.

"Correction, we *used* to date. He broke up with me."

I frowned but Killian didn't look surprised.

"When?"

"This morning," he snorted, crossing his arms over his chest which made his muscles bulge. "I called him in jail, and he hung up on me. Actually, no, he said, 'serves you right you good for nothing dolt head. We're over.' And then he spelled over like I didn't know how to spell. And *then* he hung up on me."

I blinked a few times, wondering if he was being serious or if he was joking.

"You know he's just worried. I mean, he did tell you not to get into another fight." Killian then shrugged. "He's just upset. It's his way of showing you that he cares."

"Breaking up with me is showing me that he cares?" Francisco scoffed.

★* Y.O.L.O - I.J Hidee ★*

"He does it all the time, but he always comes back to you."

"Yeah, but it's still annoying," he grumbled.

"And yet you still date him."

"Well, he's adorable. Besides, his big ego and feisty attitude makes him a perfect power bottom."

I almost choked and Killian made a face.

"Dude, TMI," he grimaced. "I'll take you to Luke's place. Seems like you two have a lot to talk about."

"What about you two? What kind of *juicy* relationship do you guys have?" Francisco asked, wriggling his eyebrows.

"We're just classmates," I answered.

"Not even friends? Ouch Jones, that actually kind of hurt," Killian chuckled dryly. Francisco then gasped.

"Kiki!" He cried, making us jump in our seats.

"What?!"

"McDonalds!" he said eagerly, pointing at the big yellow M across the road. "Can we get ice cream? Please?"

Killian's jaw tightened and he shot him a glare.

"You almost gave me a heart-attack for that?!"

"Kiki, they starved me in prison."

★* Y.O.L.O - I.J Hidee ★*

"You were in there for half a day," he deadpanned.

"Exactly!"

They started to argue. Despite their bickering, I could tell that they were best friends. I now understood why Killian said Francisco was like a brother to him.

"Jones, do you want ice cream?"

Francisco leaned towards me.

"Say that you do," he whispered into my ear.

I couldn't help but giggle.

"I do," I murmured.

"And I now pronounce you, husband and wife," Francisco declared, bopping me and Killian on the head. I couldn't stop laughing and Francisco grinned at me with a wink.
We headed to the McDonald's drive-through. Francisco and I ordered vanilla cones.

"Heaven," Francisco moaned, licking his ice-cream. "Oh sweet, sweet heaven."
I was scared that I'd drop mine, knowing how clumsy I could be, and held the cone with hands, carefully licking the vanilla flavor. A small smile lingered at the corner of Killian's lip as he looked at me with an amused look on his face.

"Does it taste good?" He asked and I bobbed my head.

"Hey, why aren't you asking me?" Francisco pouted.

"Because you've been moaning like you're having a god damn orgasm," he growled, making us both laugh.

"Are you sure you don't want any? You can have some of mine," I said to Killian, turning the cone around. "The left side is still clean. I haven't licked it yet, I promise."

"He probably didn't want one because he wanted to drive with two hands," Francisco said. "I bet he wants to keep his baby safe."

"Francis," Killian warned him.

"What? I was talking about me," Francisco said. A sly smile pulled on his lips. "Oh, you thought I was talking about Carter?"

Killian's jaw tightened but he didn't say anything. Was I going crazy or was he blushing? We drove over a road bump and a trickle of ice-cream fell between my thighs and on my seat.

I let out a small gasp. "Sorry," I said, using my sleeve to remove the stain.

"Don't do that, you'll ruin your clothes," Killian said. He put his big hands on my knee and a tingle shot down my spine. He spread my thin legs apart to get a better look at the stain.

I didn't know what I was more nervous of, the fact that he was leaning so close to me or the fact that I stained his seat. He pulled away, not mad at all.

"It's fine, it'll wash off with water," he said gently, putting both hands on the wheel when the stoplight turned green.

"Hey, how come when Carter spills something, you say it's fine, but when I drop my ketchup, you almost give me a black eye?" Francisco huffed.

"Jones is special," Killian said. I looked away, feeling my ears turn red and my heart beat faster inside my chest.

"This is Luke's place," Killian said, parking in front of a house.

"Thanks again for breaking me out of jail," Francisco said, doing a cool handshake with Killian. He looked at me with that brilliant smile of his. "I'll see you around Ma. If you ever need anything, you know where to find me!"

His bright and cheerful aura was contagious. I couldn't help but smile. He hopped out of the car and waved at us. Now that Killian and I were alone, an awkward atmosphere loomed over us.

"Carter," Killian prompted, making me flinch.

"Yes?" I squeaked, slowly turning my head towards him. But as soon as I did, he pressed his soft lips against mine and my eyes widened in shock. I felt his hand wrap around the nape of my neck as he gently pulled me closer towards him.

"You taste like ice cream," he whispered against my lips. My face burned red, and I pushed him away.

"What are you doing?" I stuttered.

He shrugged. "Sexually harassing you."

"That isn't funny," I frowned. The smile on his face disappeared, replaced by a sudden serious look.

"Jones, I know you like me. I've known for a while."

"How?" I gulped.

"Well, you literally confessed to me two hours ago," he chuckled lightly.

I squeezed my clammy hands, wanting to disappear into another universe. Then again, I did accidentally confess to him today, and I did kiss him at the party, and I did blush whenever he was around me... Gosh, how could I be so obvious?

"I know that you don't like me back," I blurted.

He gave me a quizzical look. "What?"

"You hold my hand and kiss me, but you've never asked me out. You said you knew about my feelings for a while, but you've been avoiding me at school." I bit my lower lip and took in a slow breath. "I kind of figured out that you didn't want me."

There was a look in Killian's eyes that I couldn't quite read. He was quiet for a moment, raked a hand through his hair, then finally spoke.

"I avoided you because I was scared."

"Of what?"

"Of how much I liked you."

★* Y.O.L.O - I.J Hidee ★*

My lids fluttered.

"What?"

"I avoided you because it was the first time I've felt this way about someone. When I'm with you, I realize that I'd rather make a few memories with you than a million with someone else. Everyone I've been with until now; they were all temporary passengers in my life. They come and go like ghosts. It was easier, but at the end of the day, I was alone. I felt lonely. Everything seemed meaningless."

His jaw tightened, and he stared straight ahead.

"It's like when you go to a party full of people. You know names, you know faces, but you don't really know anyone. You smile and chat, drink and have fun, but wake up the next day with nothing but a few blurry memories of someone you'll forget in a week."

Killian looked at me and my chest tightened.

"But you? I don't want you to be someone I forget in a few days, or a week, or even in a few months. I want you to stay," he said. His beautiful green eyes captivated me as he spoke. "And I'm scared, Jones. I'm scared of being in a relationship, of giving myself to someone and letting someone give themselves to me. That's a big responsibility and I'm not sure if I'm ready for it, but I'd rather look back at my life and say, 'I'm glad I tried,' instead of saying, 'I wish I'd tried.' To hell with playing it safe."

He smiled at me, and his eyes never looked brighter than they did now.

"So, Carter Jones, what do you say?" he asked. "Will you be my boyfriend?"

He looked both nervous and hopeful, and I realized that there was no such thing as being completely ready. But if you got to point in your life where you felt more excited than afraid, that was when you went for it. That was when you went all in. You took your chances in hopes to turn a risk into something much more beautiful.

"Yes," I beamed. "Of course I'll be your boyfriend."

★* Y.O.L.O - I.J Hidee ★*

Chapter 30: Two Bad Boys in a Room

"Dinner is in the fridge. Your dad and I are working a nightshift tonight, so we won't be back until morning," Mom said. I looked up from my flashcards and nodded.

"Oh, and Carter?"

"Yeah?"

Her eyes softened and she gave me a small smile.

"Don't push yourself," she murmured, and this time, I knew she meant it. I smiled back.

"I won't," I promised.

She gave me a quick kiss on the head before closing the door behind her. When her footsteps got further, I quickly turned the lock.

"Pssst. Is the cost clear?" someone whispered. A smile grew on my face.

"All good!" I replied. Killian crawled through the open window and hopped into my room. He straightened his clothes and ran a hand through his hair. He looked immaculate.

"Hi," he said. I jumped into his arms, smiling so hard my face felt like it could rip. He chuckled softly into my hair, squeezing me tightly against him.

"Hey," I said, digging my face against his chest and taking a whiff of his addicting scent. I pulled away and looked up at him.

"You could have used the front door," I said.

"Wait, so you're telling me I climbed up your roof and almost risked breaking a leg for nothing?" he gasped playfully. He tapped my nose. "Well, it would have been worth it."

He lowered his head, his lips brushing against mine. I looped my hands around his neck to deepen the kiss. His tongue entered my mouth and he fumbled for my belt. There was a tightness in my stomach.

"Wait," I gasped.

"What's wrong?" he asked, his eyebrows pulling together in worry.

"Are we going to do it?"

He blinked blankly before bursting into laughter, making me turn bright red.

"What?" I huffed with a pout.

"Nothing, nothing," he chuckled, pressing his forehead against mine. His face was so close, I had to fight the temptation to kiss him. "It's just that people normally don't ask before actually doing it."

"Oh," I said, embarrassed. He tilted his head and kissed my neck. I shivered with pleasure, tightening my grip around him. The warmth of his tongue made me feel hot.

"We don't have to if you don't want to," he murmured.

"No, I want to—" before I could finish my sentence, he pushed me onto the bed, pulling his shirt over his head.

"Say no more," he said with a wolfish grin and hungry eyes.

"What happened to your modesty?" I chuckled nervously.

He shrugged. "I got tired of being good."

I grinned.

"Me too."

I laughed when his mouth locked with mine. He gently pushed me onto my back. Everything happened so quickly, by the time my eyes fluttered open, our clothes were on the floor, and I was wearing nothing but a shirt.

"Killian," I said nervously. "This is my first time."

"Tell me if I'm going too fast." His husky voice sent chills down my spine, and I nodded with a gulp. His big hand skimmed up the inner part of my sigh and I moaned at the sensation that sprung through my body. He unbuttoned my shirt, but I guess he was desperate to get my clothes off. He ripped open my shirt and the buttons flew everywhere. I don't think I've ever been so terrified yet, attracted to someone before.

He kissed my nipple, pressing his tongue against it before biting it while rubbing the other with his thumb. My eyes rolled back, and I moaned in pleasure, my hands getting lost in his hair as he rolled the erect bead against his tongue. My lower member started to swell. He rubbed against me, and my pulse went crazy. When his hand glided down the flat of my stomach and closer to my erection, I stopped breathing.

"Do you want me to stop?" he asked.

"No, don't stop," I said, almost in a begging voice. Killian slipped his fingers into my mouth. I held onto his wrist with both hands, my member getting excited as I started to suck, feeling his index and middle finger twirl around my tongue. He put a finger inside of me. I whimpered, digging my nails into his back at the sensation.

His hand began to move in and out, and I moved my hips to the rhythm. He inserted another finger and my back arched. He pumped harder and deeper each time. The third one hurt the most, especially when he parted his fingers to widen my hole. The tingling sensation of both pain and pleasure had my back arched and my teeth sunk into my lower lip. He then moved his hand to my erection, and I moaned.
My toes curled and my back arched, my breath quickening after each stroke, every nerve in my body and brain feeling electrified as he quickened his pace, using my precum to his advantage.

The ache in my lower abdomen worsened and I wanted to cum. He moved his thumb in slow, circular motions. Right when I was about to reach climax, he pressed his finger against the tip.

"Not yet," he whispered huskily into my ear. He pulled his fingers out and took a condom out of his pant pockets. He ripped it open, and it was only when he fit his erection into it that I realized how big he was. My jaw dropped. "Killian!"

He looked startled. "What's wrong?"

"That is never going to fit me."

He blinked then barked into laughter, and I felt a wave of nervousness rush through me.

"Trust me, we'll make it work," he winked. I always got nervous and excited when he said we. I gasped when he entered me, clinging so tightly only his back that I could hardly feel my fingers.

"Shit, Jones, you're so tight," I heard him mutter. He pushed himself all the way in and I felt my insides stretch.

"Is that a bad thing?" I whimpered.

"No, it's perfect."

A breathy noise slipped out of my mouth when he started to push in and out. Our bodies rocked back and forth, causing the bed to creak as his hips moved. His breathing became ragged and heavy, and I could feel the tension rippling through his muscles. I could tell he was trying his hardest to be gentle with me and that he was fighting back the temptation to go quicker, harder, and rougher.

"Killian," I whispered against his mouth. "Make me feel good."

His eyes widened followed by a smile. And a beast was released. I didn't know the mistake I made until he grabbed my hips and pushed so deep into me, I felt his erection all the way to my throat. Strained moans escaped my lips, and I felt an unexplainable pleasure rip through me. I could hear his waist slap against my butt, tears forming in my eyes as I cried his name endlessly. I tried to cover my face, but Killian pinned my wrists above my head.

"Sorry, Jones, you're going to have to let me be selfish with you," he grunted, thrusting into me. "I really want to see you cry."

We continued to kiss and grope, thrust and tease, his tip growing bigger and bigger inside of me, hitting a sensitive area that made me moan his name louder. My legs started to shake uncontrollably as I hit climax. But Killian didn't stop there. He removed his condom, putting his erection against mine and pumping them together with his hand. My breath quickened and my back arched. We both climaxed, cumming simultaneously. Killian plopped on top of me, our bodies still shaking with pleasure. We laid there, breathless.

Killian pulled me closer against him and I rested my head on his chest. I could hear his heart racing inside his chest and smiled when he planted a kiss on my head. I closed my eyes to savor this perfect moment.

★* Y.O.L.O - I.J Hidee ★*

Chapter 31: The Last Dare

My eyes fluttered open. It took me a few seconds to grasp reality. Night had fallen, and the moon cast a beam of light through my window. I blinked a few times, wondering if I was in a dream. But my memories slowly started to recollect. I frantically sat up and looked around me, but my bed was empty. I felt the blood in my face drain down my neck as panic hammered against my chest.

"Killian?"

No answer.

I swallowed the lump in my throat. He was gone. Killian was really gone. Where did he go? Did he leave after we slept together? Without telling me or saying goodbye?

My chest tightened.

Was he already tired of me? He wouldn't cast me aside after one night, would he?

I hugged my knees tightly against my chest. I closed my eyes and shook my head.

★* Y.O.L.O - I.J Hidee ★*

No, Killian wasn't like that. He wasn't a bad person.

I scrambled out of bed but yelped when I felt a jolt of pain shoot up my waist. I bit my lower lip with a frown.

Jenna was right. Killian really was a beast in the sheets.

I took in a shaky breath and managed to go downstairs. The house was dark and silent. I checked the most plausible places he could be. I went to the living room and bathroom — they were empty.

My chest tightened every time I opened a door to find the room empty. I refused to believe that he left without a word. I refused to believe that everything was a lie. I refused to believe that he had used me. Killian wasn't a bad person. He wasn't.

But I couldn't find him. I stopped and tilted my head back against the wall, trying to steady my shaky breaths. Water formed in my eyes and the world went blurry. But then I heard a noise coming from the kitchen. I dashed down the hallway, my eyes widening.

Killian was leaning against the counter, one hand pressed against the sink, another holding a glass of water. He wore nothing but his pants and an unbuttoned shirt. The silver light that spilled through the room danced on his smooth, olive skin, defining the shadows and lines of his muscles. He pushed back his dark hair, staring out the window. Even at night, his eyes were beautiful.

When he took a sip of water, he noticed me standing at the entrance. His eyes widened in surprise, then turned into an expression of worry.

"Jones?" He put the cup down and came over to me, gently raising my chin. "Why are you crying?"

"Sorry," I said with a shaky laugh. "I um, I had a bad dream."

But Killian knew that I was lying. He frowned, but instead of drowning me with questions, he wrapped his strong arms around me and planted a kiss on my head. His embrace felt warm and soothing.

"I thought you left," I said in a shaky voice.

"Is that why you're crying?" he chuckled softly, more amused than upset. He brushed away the last of my tears, the cold metal of his rings touching my skin. "I was thirsty and came down to get some water. You were sleeping so peacefully; I didn't want to wake you."

I felt embarrassed and stared at my toes. "Oh."

"I know I'm not perfect," Killian said, his voice hoarse and soft all at once. "Knowing me, I'm probably going to make mistakes. Lots of them. But fuck, I like you too much to be selfless."

He was always honest, someone who spoke his thoughts whenever he needed or wanted to.

"What if I hurt you?" he whispered.

I wanted him to know that he wasn't alone on this. I ran my hand along his biceps. His eyes closed at my touch.

"Ask me a question," I murmured.

"What do you want me to ask?"

"Anything but that," I giggled, using the answer he once gave me. He smiled.

"Here, I'll help," I said. "Ask me what I like about you."

"What do you like about me?" he mused.

"I don't know if I have an answer for that," I admitted.

He stared at me, confused.

"I don't have an answer, but I have a few that might give you an idea. You're smart, you're crazy, and you're spontaneous. You're different, and I don't say that because it's cliche. I've never met someone who kicks vending machines for strangers, or who dumps spaghetti on people out of the blue, and I definitely have never met someone who calls the principal Mr. Roro like he's a bro." He laughed at that. "And I don't think I'll meet ever meet someone who asks me to break his best friend out of jail either."

His smile broadened.

"You're the most amazing, craziest person I've met. You're full of life. I guess that's what I like about you."

The way Killian looked deeply into my eyes, listening to every word I said, made me feel shy and embarrassed. Even though it was just the two of us, I felt like the entire world could hear me. But I knew I needed to tell him— No, that I *wanted* to tell him how I felt. I was tired of being scared, of holding myself back, of making choices I'd regret.

★* Y.O.L.O - I.J Hidee ★*

I took his hand, the one with the tattoo that started it all.

"I'm scared too," I finally said. "But fuck it, right?" His eyes widened in shock. "I want us to live life like we only have one. So what if we make mistakes? Y.O.L.O, right?"

Killian smiled. He lifted me into his arms and spun me around. I laughed as the world around us blurred. He stopped and his eyes focused on me, and his lips pressed against mine. When he pulled away, his green eyes sparkled.

"Y.O.L.O," he murmured.

★* Y.O.L.O - I.J Hidee ★*

Book #2 – W.O.L.O
We Only Live Once

Written in Killian's POV, don't miss out on Killian and Carter's adventures in the sequel to the Y.O.L.O series.

W.O.L.O

Chapter 1: Better

I sunk my teeth into my lower lip as Jones sucked. I tilted my head back, my grip tightening around the steering wheel. We were parked in an empty parking lot. Not the most romantic place, I know, but it was our go-to when we were horny. Well, when I was horny.

His tongue swirled around my tip. I tried my best not to swear in front of him, *but holy shit has he gotten better.*

I ran my hand through his soft, brown hair, my breath ragged at the warmth of his mouth. He looked up through his long lashes, his warm chestnut eyes making my heart melt. I cupped his face in my hands, tilting his chin up.

"Does your jaw hurt?" I asked gently.

"My mouth is too small," he murmured sheepishly. He averted his eyes to the side, pursing his lips. "And... You're too big."

I let out a small chuckle. I didn't want to sound arrogant, but I had to admit that his words boosted my ego.

"Do you want to go deeper?" I asked before I could stop myself.

"Will it hurt?" The look he gave me was so innocent and pure, I couldn't help but feel a pang of guilt hit my chest. I felt like I was corrupting an angel.

"You don't have to if-"

"N-No, I want to!" He blurted. I raised my brows and his cheeks flushed red in embarrassment. I parted my lips, but I was cut off by a strained grunt when Jones put my erection back into his mouth. I hissed at the pleasure.

We fooled around in my jeep until an alarm interrupted us. Jones always set an alarm because he knew we'd lose track of time if he didn't. We probably would never stop if the annoying ringing noise didn't snap us out of it. I buckled my belt and he put on his shirt.

"Do we have to go?" I mumbled.
"It's 7:40. School is going to start soon," he chuckled. That was another thing I needed to get used to. Going to school on time. I would have normally tried to

convince my partner to stay a little longer. Maybe I could change his mind with a few kisses and cuddles, all it would take-

No Killian, get your shit together. This is Jones we're talking about.

"Right," I grunted, pushing away my thoughts. I zipped up my pants, put on my seatbelt, and stepped on the pedal.

"How's your throat?" I asked worriedly.

"It's still a little sore," he admitted, rubbing his neck. "Did I do okay?"

"Okay?" I laughed. "You were amazing."

His eyes widened and he swiveled his head the other way, gluing his nose to the window. His ears were bright red.

"T-T-Thank you, you did a good job too!"

I barked into laughter.

"A good job?" I echoed. He nodded, nervously fiddling with his sleeves. There was nothing more satisfying than seeing someone you liked wearing your oversized hoodie.

I wanted to hold his hand but remembered that I needed two hands on the wheels. That was another thing. Ever since Jones and I started dating, I noticed I was changing. I partied less, drank less, smoked less, because yes, I went back to the habit of smoking. I went to school, not always, but at least I tried I still sucked at studying, but Jones would help me with that. My C's turned into B's, and I haven't missed a single test since. I still got into trouble, and I wasn't exactly *good*. just better.

And I realized that was the biggest difference between Jones and the other people I've dated.

Everyone else tried to change me. He made me want to change.

Jones' life had also altered. He went out more, met new people, and made more friends; Francisco and my mom being two of them. Mom would often invite him over for dinner without even asking me.

Francisco adored him too, and the three of us would hang out after school. Luke would be there too sometimes when he didn't have football practice. Luke didn't have much of an opinion on Jones and Jones was still scared of him. Even though he was my best friend, I knew that Luke wasn't always easy to get along with. Fortunately, Francisco was there to break the ice.

Overall, Carter had changed. He was still the straight-A student I knew when I first met him, but happier.

★* Y.O.L.O - I.J Hidee ★*

The ride to school was short. The parking lot was almost full by the time we arrived, and I could already see a few cars circle around to find a parking spot. I didn't have to look and parked my jeep in my usual spot. You had to come to school extra early if you wanted to find the best spots with shade and space, but this one was reserved for me. It was known as my parking spot, one of the perks of being popular.

Carter undid his seatbelt and picked up his bag. I remained in my seat, my car key still in the initiator. We had a two-minute rule. Carter left first, and I'd leave two minutes after him. As much as I wanted to scream to the world that this precious boy was mine, especially to Casper who he's been hanging around a lot, Jones and I decided that it was best if we kept our relationship lowkey.

He hadn't told Eshe yet. I could tell his best friend didn't like me that much. Whenever she saw me with Jones, she'd shoot me a nasty glare. Not that it mattered or anything. I'd just smile and give her a quick wink before going on with the rest of my day.

Even if Jones came out to his parents, he wasn't ready for the entire school to know. I respected that decision, and even if I wanted to hold his hand or kiss him in the hallways, I agreed that it might be best if we kept our relationship a secret.

People would spread nasty rumors and jealousy could get ugly. Lots of girls I've dated in the past were harassed by my crazy ex's. Who knows what they'd do to Jones? *My* Jones?

As confident as I was, I didn't know if I could protect him from an angry army of cheerleaders or a mob of pissed-off jocks. Before him, I slept around a lot, which meant that I had several enemies who'd leap at the chance to get revenge on me. Take Jenna as exhibit A.

"Thanks for driving me to school," he said, snapping me out of my thoughts.

"Always," I smiled, pushing away my worries. Wait, since when did I worry?

Since you started caring, said a voice in the back of my head.

Great.

He gave me a small wave and closed the door behind him. I frowned, feeling disappointed. My jeep suddenly felt empty. But a few seconds later, the door opened again, and my eyebrows quirked. Jones leaned forward, wrapping his hand around the nape of my neck, giving me a quick peck on the lips. My eyes widened and he gave me a shy smile when he pulled away.

"Sorry, I forgot your goodbye kiss," he stammered, blushing furiously. "Okay, bye!"

★* Y.O.L.O - I.J Hidee ★*

He closed the door and I watched him dash into the school, almost tripping on his way. I sat there, speechless, then groaned, slamming my head against the steering wheel, and accidentally honking the horn.

I raked a hand through my dark hair, closing my eyes with a stupid smile on my face.

I was falling way too hard for this boy.

Printed in Great Britain
by Amazon